MW01200112

ARTHUR'S HONOR

THE AEGIS NETWORK: JACKSONVILLE DIVISION

JEN TALTY

JUPITER PRESS

PRAISE FOR JEN TALTY

"Deadly Secrets is the best of romance and suspense in one hot read!" *NYT Bestselling Author Jennifer Probst*

"A charming setting and a steamy couple heat up the pages in a suspenseful story I couldn't put down!" *NY Times and USA today Bestselling Author Donna Grant*

"Jen Talty's books will grab your attention and pull you into a world of relatable characters, strong personalities, humor, and believable storylines. You'll laugh, you'll cry, and you'll rush to get the next book she releases!" Natalie Ann USA Today Bestselling Author

"I positively loved *In Two Weeks*, and highly recommend it. The writing is wonderful, the story is fantastic, and the characters will keep you coming back for more. I can't wait to get my hands on future installments of the NYS Troopers series." *Long and Short Reviews*

"*In Two Weeks* hooks the reader from page one. This is a fast paced story where the development of the romance grabs you emotionally and the suspense keeps you sitting on the edge of your chair. Great characters, great writing, and a believable plot that can be a warning to all of us." *Desiree Holt, USA Today Bestseller*

"*Dark Water* delivers an engaging portrait of wounded hearts as the memorable characters take you on a healing journey of love. A mysterious death brings danger and intrigue into the drama, while sultry passions brew into a believable plot that melts the reader's heart. Jen Talty pens an entertaining romance that grips the heart as the colorful and dangerous story unfolds into a chilling ending." *Night Owl Reviews*

"This is not the typical love story, nor is it the typical mystery. The characters are well rounded and interesting." *You Gotta Read Reviews*

"Murder in Paradise Bay is a fast-paced romantic thriller with plenty of twists and turns to keep you guessing until the end. You won't want to miss this one..." *USA Today bestselling author Janice Maynard*

Two lives, one conspiracy: unraveling the truth could cost them everything.

After a mission gone wrong, Arthur Knight and his team find themselves in a new, secretive world. Recruited by an old friend into the elite Aegis Network, they are promised not only the benefits of military service but also access to crucial information that could help Arthur unravel a lingering mystery from his past.

Maren Cordelia's life takes a dramatic turn when she's involved in a car accident while on her way home to assist her mother with a business deal. Saved by a stranger, she's eager to express her gratitude, but the rescuer is reluctant to have any involvement with her or her apology. However, a string of suspicious incidents, including a fire in the marina, forced Arthur and his team to investigate matters more closely.

Together, Arthur and Maren embark on a treacherous journey where trust is a rare commodity, and the truth could be more perilous than the lies they're unraveling.

NOTE FROM THE AUTHOR

Hello everyone!

It is important to note that this book was originally titled *Burning Desire* and written as part of the Susan Stoker *Special Forces: Operation Alpha* world. Since the rights to the book have reverted back to me, I have stripped the story of all the elements from Susan's world (as it was legally required of me to do so) as well as changing the names of some of my characters so it would fit nicely into my Aegis Network series.

I have also expanded the story, adding scenes and updating a few things. I'm much happier with the storyline and characters now. I've always loved this series, but as with many things that I wrote years ago, I felt as though I could have done better.

Please enjoy!
Jen Talty

To the Crew on Smile Maker. You know where the Wreck on the Rocks are!

WELCOME TO THE AEGIS NETWORK

The Aegis Network is the brainchild of former Marines, Bain Asher and Decker Griggs. While serving their country, Bain and Decker were injured in a raid in an undisclosed area during an unsanctioned mission. Instead of twiddling their thumbs while on medical leave, they focused their frustration at being sidelined toward their pet project: a sophisticated Quantum Communication Network Satellite. When the devastating news came that neither man would be placed on active duty ever again, they sold their technology to the United States government and landed on a heaping pot of gold and funded their passion.

Saving lives.

The Aegis Network is an elite group of men and women, mostly ex-military, descending from all branches. They may have left the armed forces, but the armed forces didn't leave them. There's no limit to the type of missions they'll take, from kidnapping, protection detail, infiltrating enemy lines, and everything in between; no job is too big or too small when lives are at stake.

As Marines, they vowed no man left behind.

As civilians, they will risk all to ensure the safety of their clients.

A Note From Jen Talty

Some researchers have said there is a correlation between the ocean and being calm, happier, and more creative. Having spent a winter in Jupiter, Florida, I'd say these researchers are right on the money.

The SARICH BROTHERS series was born while I spent four months in Jupiter, walking the beach, visiting the Jupiter Lighthouse, driving around Jupiter Island, dining at various places on the water, and overall enjoying this next chapter in my life known as the 'empty nest.'

The Sarich brothers, while poor, had a good life, raised by loving parents. However, their father was killed in the line of duty when the oldest boy was just twenty and the youngest fourteen, changing their lives forever...

Each of the brothers struggle with a restlessness, in part caused by their father's death. They are strong, honorable, and loyal men. They aren't looking for a woman, as their jobs aren't necessarily conducive with long-term relationships. It's going to take an equally strong woman to rip down the Sarich brothers' defenses and help them settle their restlessness, so they can give their hearts.

The series does not need to be read in order, but the four novellas do follow a timeline.

Come join each of the Sarich boys in their journey to heal old wounds, mend broken hearts, and find their way to true happiness with the love of a good, strong woman.

I want to add that since this series has been released, and then re-released, my readers, have begged me to write Mrs. Sarich's story...well, it's coming! Look for Catherine's story, THE MATRI-ARCH, on January 14, 2020.

*Sign up for Jen's Newsletter (*https://dl.bookfunnel.com/rg8mx9lchy*) where she often gives away free books before publication.*

*Join Jen's private Facebook group (*https://www.facebook.com/groups/191706547909047/*), where she posts exclusive excerpts and discusses all things murder and love!*

Book Description

Ramey Sarich graduated from West Point Military Academy with honors and a broken heart. Swearing off relationships, but not women, he dives into his career as a test pilot for the Army. He's cocky and lives on the edge, but he knows he's the best test pilot the Army has ever seen. So, when one of the planes he's testing nearly crashes, he doesn't believe it was an accident. Wanting an outside source, he contacts his brothers, and they send help in the form of an ex-military female pilot now part of the AEGIS NETWORK. Ramey is prepared for anything, except Tequila Ryder.

Tequila Ryder has spent the last few years raising her half-sister's son. Now that he's settled in college, Tequila is eager to jump back in the field with the

AEGIS NETWORK. She's dealt with more than one arrogant pilot before; however, Ramey is anything but typical, and as she dives into the investigation, she can only come to two conclusions.

Either someone is trying to destroy Ramey's career.

Or kill him.

…together they unravel a twisted plot, while entangling their hearts, and falling hard. Hopefully they won't crash and burn both in the sky and in love.

———

"Here's to getting back alive." Arthur Knight raised his drink and made sure to clank every single one of his team's shot glasses before tapping it on the table and bringing it to his lips. He jerked his head back and swallowed the tequila in a single gulp. "How were things at the station while Rex and I were gone?" When Arthur left the Air Force four months ago, six other men from his fire protection specialist team joined him without even asking.

"Quiet," Hawke said.

"One actual fire call and the rest were your standard non-fire emergencies but exactly what we called upon for every single day." Buddy reached across the table and snagged one of Kent's onion rings before Kent moved his plate from Buddy's grasp. "Working for a local fire station sure differs from being employed by the Air Force."

"After that last mission blew up in our faces." Duncan rubbed his shoulder. "I'm sure as shit glad to have walked away when we did." I'm still not a hundred percent and not sure I ever will be."

"None of us got our twenty years in, which I personally get shit for," Garth, the youngest of the group, said. "But to be fair, some of the shit that Asher and Griggs have us doing isn't any easier than what we did in the military."

"Can't say being a regular firefighter is either." Kent arched a brow. "But I ain't complaining. Especially since I get to do it with you assholes."

"Cheers to that." Arthur sipped his beer. Leaving the Air Force at thirty-six hadn't been part of Arthur's life plan. Far from it. He loved serving his country. It had given him purpose after his life had turned upside down.

First by tragedy.

Then by divorce.

However, when an old buddy approached him and his team with a job opportunity that would not only give him a similar career path but also the freedom to settle his soul, he took it. All he had to do was talk his team into taking the leap with him and moving from Cape Canaveral to Jacksonville.

"Speaking of which, both Rex and I have three days off from the station." He waggled his finger. "Some of you idiots are on the schedule tomorrow at the station."

"Sometimes this schedule is more grueling than when we were in the Air Force." Buddy pounded back his beer. "Except I like Jacksonville better, and to be fair, the rotation schedule is so much better."

"Not to mention we're not deployed for weeks or months, with no clue as to where we're going or when we're coming home." Garth laughed. "One of us might actually get married."

"I already did that once." Arthur would often like to forget his short-lived marriage. It wasn't that he didn't love her, because he did. But his past always got in the way. "I don't ever plan on doing it again."

"Never say never," Kent, the only father in the group, said. Leaving the military had been an easy choice for Kent. Being a single dad, he had one foot out the door when Arthur approached him with the idea. The move had proved to be a blessing for him and his daughter. He glanced at his watch. "I've got to go relieve my sitter. I'll see you all later."

"Take it easy, man." Arthur nodded.

Rex jerked his head. "Hey, isn't that Mrs. Cordelia?"

Arthur glanced over his shoulder. "It is. But who is that man she's with?" Arthur kept his boat in the Cordelia Marina. He spent a fair amount of time with Mrs. Cordelia, a sweet older widow who brought him homemade cookies and let him borrow her dog.

"I'm pretty sure I've seen him in this bar before, but I don't know who he is," Buddy said.

"I'm a little surprised to see her in this place." Arthur smiled in her direction. "Although, they look cozy. Like they're on a date." That warmed his heart. She deserved a little happiness in her life.

"They do appear smitten, and this is the perfect place to take a lady if you want to impress her with the local fish and a good band," Garth said.

Hawke burst out laughing. "Please tell me this is not the joint you're taking the chicks you date, because if it is, we need to up your game."

Garth wadded up a napkin and tossed it at Hawke. "I meant to say for a people their age. If I'm going out, it will be downtown to a club or that new place, Roadies."

"I was there the other night. They had a rockin' band," Hawke said. "Amazing."

Arthur was getting too old for any of that shit. Sometimes he felt as though parts of his life had passed him by. He'd been in love before. Twice.

Married once.

That had been a total bust.

They had started out strong, but she soon wanted him to give up the Air Force, among other things. The time hadn't been right, but he wasn't opposed to the conversation, especially when discussions of a family were involved.

But that dream died before it began.

And he didn't see it being rejuvenated.

Mrs. Cordelia strolled across the room. "Arthur. It's so good to see you. I thought you were out of town on an assignment with the Aegis Network."

"I just returned a few hours ago." He rose, taking her hand and kissing the back of it. She reminded him of his mom, a woman he missed more than life.

"Did I tell you that my Maren is coming into town? You two are finally going to meet."

He resisted the urge to roll his eyes. Mrs. Cordelia had been chatting up her lovely daughter for months. It was all she could talk about.

That and Maren's shitty boyfriend.

Two things Arthur didn't get involved in were chicks who were already spoken for.

And nice older ladies who tried to set them up with their daughters.

"You mentioned it."

"She'll be here sometime tomorrow. I hope you'll stop by so I can introduce you."

His first thought was to give her a million excuses as to why he wouldn't be able to; only he had every intention of being at that marina. "I'm sure our paths will cross while she's here."

"Well, I'd better get back to my friend." She patted his hand. "I made freshly baked cookies, so be sure to stop by before they're all gone."

"Will do." He kissed her cheek. "You take care, now." He eased back into his seat. "If I had a dollar for every time that woman has mentioned her daughter to me, I'd be a rich man."

"Aren't you the least bit curious?" Rex asked. "I don't think you've taken out a single woman since we moved here."

"Not even a little bit." Arthur reached in his back pocket and pulled out his wallet. "I think it's time I call it a night. I've got a date with some fish in the morning." He tossed a couple of twenties on the table. Now that he'd left the military, he found his idle mind wandering to his past a little more than he'd like. In the last six months, he'd spent more time searching for answers to a mystery that had left an entire family dead.

And his heart shattered.

2

"Mom, I don't mind." Maren Cordelia glanced in the rearview mirror. The same asshole had been riding her bumper for the last five minutes. She put on her blinker and moved to the left lane.

"What about your job, dear?"

Maren's heart lurched to the center of her throat. No way could she tell her mother that she'd quit. Five years ago, she'd made a huge fuss about not wanting to stay and work in the family business and ran off for the hustle and bustle of New York City to be a chief risk officer on Wall Street.

Of course, that also had to do with the jerk of a boyfriend she'd followed from her hometown of

Jacksonville, Florida, to the Big Apple. What a mistake that had been.

"I told you, I've got a few weeks of vacation time built up. I'm happy to come home and help you figure this out."

"What about Tom? Why isn't he coming down with you?"

"He's got too much going on right now." She knew she'd eventually have to tell her mother the truth. However, her top priority was convincing her mom to sell the marina and not take on an investor who seemed too good to be anything other than a con artist. Once she did that, she could tell her mother about the breakup and her job.

"I could have just sent you all the paperwork. I do know how to scan and use email. I'm even doing Instagram and Facebook right on my phone. I might even give TikTok a try."

Her mother had fought technology until the love of her life had died. Maren had hooked her up with accounts and found many of her old high school friends and family members, giving her mother a way to communicate and do something other than crying.

Now, Maren almost wished she'd never helped

her mother set all that up because she was always posting, all day long.

"I want to meet this person and discuss the details. Make sure it's the right decision for you." Maren veered toward the exit ramp, her GPS indicating she was fifteen minutes from the marina, which she knew, so why she had the damn thing on, she had no idea.

"I see. Well, you walked away from this marina and your heritage. I don't need your permission to bring on a partner." Her mother's voice took on that tone of indignation that Maren hated.

"Mom. I'm just trying to help. You do remember what happened to Mrs. Baxter, right?"

"Are you trying to lump me in with that old loon? Not only is she crazy, but she's not the smartest woman either. I would never fall for a scam like that. I'm insulted."

"I didn't mean it that way." Even if Maren had said it differently, her mother would have taken it ass-backward. She always did, especially lately. "Besides, I haven't been home since Daddy died and that was two years ago. I miss you, Mom."

A long sigh echoed over the speaker. "I miss you too, little one. I don't like the way things have been between us lately."

"Neither do I," Maren said. "Please understand that I'm only trying to do what Daddy would have expected of me."

"I know, little one. When will you be here? I've got fresh cookies with your name on them. Though I do have to save some for that cute Aegis Network agent I told you about. He's back from a recent mission and has a few days off. Maybe you'll finally get to meet him."

Maren rolled her eyes. Her mom had never liked Tom. Not even when he'd been sweet and kind. God, she'd been a fool. He'd been cheating on her the entire time, and she'd been too stupid to see it. Tom had swept her off her feet and made her feel special. He bought her gifts all the time. Little did she know they were guilt presents for every time he was with another woman.

It had been six months since she'd told Tom to take his cheating ways somewhere else. And he'd sent her a dozen roses every Friday for the last six months. Every Monday, he'd send her tulips. On Wednesday, he'd call and leave a message.

With every note, voicemail, or text, he'd tell her how sorry he was, how he'd never do it again, and how much he loved her.

And every Saturday, someone would snap a

picture of her ex-boyfriend with a bimbo on his arm at some club or sucking face with some chick. The one time she answered his call, telling him she'd seen him out on the town, flaunting his latest flame, his comment had been, "I was fixed up. I didn't want to go, but babe, if you came back to me, then all of that would stop."

Yeah, right.

Now she'd have to listen to her mother tell her *I told you so, and oh, let me fix you up with Arthur. He's ex-military and he's a stand-up guy*. Well, no, thank you. Maren wasn't having anything to do with men for a long while. She didn't care about their background or who spoke up for their character.

"I'll be there in fifteen minutes," Maren said. "Love you, Mom." She tapped the end button on the phone and cranked up the tunes. Even if she did want to start dating again, it would never be a military man. Not even one who'd left the military. She'd done that once, and she swore she'd never do it again. Those types of men were too rigid. Too set in their ways. And they tended to live off adrenaline rushes, and she preferred a quiet evening in front of the fire with a glass of wine.

Then again, she thought New York would be her special place, but she'd hated it the moment she set foot in the city. She knew it would be different from her sleepy seaside town outside of Jacksonville, and she had looked forward to the hustle and bustle of the big city. She had dreamed of living there since she could remember but it hadn't been anything as she had expected. She felt invisible. She would step out of her apartment, into the sea of people, and disappear. No one looked you in the eye. No one said hello. She was a cog in a big machine she didn't even understand. She was lost and alone, and Tom did nothing to help her fit in. If anything, he made her feel more like an outsider.

She rolled to a stop at the corner of Garner and Endicott, about five miles from the marina, and decided to pull into Mr. O'Leary's Bait and Tackle shop where you could also get the best damn home-made ice cream known to man.

She parked her car between two pickups. Tom would have had gone ballistic, all worried her doors would get dented. As much as she hated to admit it, sitting between a white truck and a dark-blue one, she sort of worried about her compact car getting a nick or two.

The store hadn't changed one bit over the years. Same white sign that read Welcome to O'Leary's Bait and Tackle hung proudly over the front door, which sported that gross pastel-blue color that stuck out like a sore thumb. The bell over the door dinged as she entered. To the left was the tackle shop and to the right, the entryway to pure fat heaven.

God, she missed this quaint little town.

Jacksonville itself could be considered a big city, by Florida standards. It had a Naval and Air Force Base. There was a fair amount of traffic, especially by the beaches, including her family's marina. But these little local hidden gems made that all worth the minor hassles of dealing with dozens of red lights and tons of vehicles. And it was nothing like New York City. That place was awful.

"Well, looky what the manatee dragged in," Shea O'Leary said. She'd been a year younger than Maren, but they bonded over having to work for their family's businesses. They'd discussed leaving town many nights over a cold Corona, swearing they'd never take over for their parents. Many local children wanted the hell out. They wanted to see the world. Go to places they'd never been instead of being stuck doing the same thing their parents and grandparents had done.

This was especially true when so many businesses were seasonal or relied heavily on tourism, the few snowbirds who came to northern Florida, or the military families who were in and out.

"Long time no see." Maren took her old friend in a warm embrace, and they held each other for a good minute. "I have to say, I'm a little surprised to see you here. Last I heard, you were living in Georgia."

"That didn't last very long," Shea said. "I moved back about a year ago." She let out a short laugh. "I own this place now, but my folks won't fully retire, nor will they stop telling me what to do."

"Hence the blue and orange décor hasn't changed."

"Oh, that will change when they visit my uncle in two weeks. When they come back, this place will look entirely different."

"Thank God." When Maren and Shea were kids, they constantly talked about how ugly the typical Florida colors were and how all the places around here needed an update.

"What brings you back to town?" Shea asked as she moved behind the counter, opening the lid on the ice cream cabinet and pointing to the double chocolate chip.

Maren nodded, her mouth watering in anticipation. "Some guy named Hudson Nally wants to become partners with my mother, and it worries me."

"I've heard of him." Shea piled the ice cream into a sugar cone. "He's making offers like that up and down the shoreline."

"What do you think about him?"

Shea shrugged. "He came in here, and I didn't let him give me his pitch, so I have no opinion, but Lester Holt, I think, is taking him up on his offer."

"Mother's is still in business?" Everyone in this area avoided Mother's. Besides attracting undesirables of all kinds, the food and service had been horrible. Of course, there had always been rumors that the back room was used for sex for hire by the waitresses. To her knowledge, no one had ever been busted.

"I think they are on the verge of bankruptcy, so I have no idea why anyone would want to invest in them."

Maren could think of a few reasons, the first one being Mother's sat on a prime real estate location and in this town, location was everything.

"Hey, do you mind?" a male voice boomed across the room. "I'm in a hurry here."

"I'll be right with you." Shea handed Maren the

ice cream cone and leaned in. "This guy comes here every day. He's always in a hurry and can be a bit terse if there's a line, but don't you think he's hot?"

Maren glanced over her shoulder. The man was a tad older and had a buzzcut, but she couldn't deny the gentleman had swagger.

"If he ever comes in here in a halfway decent mood, I'm going to ask him out," Shea whispered.

"I'm a paying customer, not some old girlfriend to gossip with," the man said with an arched brow and a half-cocked smile.

Maren leaned against the counter, enjoying the calories that would go straight to her hips, watching Shea deal with the not-so-angry customer who lamely attempted to flirt.

Shea had long blond hair, almond-colored eyes, and a body that looked like it belonged on the cover of a surfer magazine. Shea had always turned heads. And this guy was no exception. His frustration wasn't that he was in a hurry, but that he wanted his five minutes with Shea.

The man said thank you and headed out the door just as another gentleman approached the counter.

Maren could only see his backside, and oh, did

this one have a nice ass, with his jeans hanging loose and low on his hips.

And he sported flip-flops. For whatever reason, she loved that look on a man.

He turned and she swallowed her breath. This man was stunningly gorgeous.

"I've got to get going. I'll see you later." Maren waved, trying not to eye the man candy at the counter with his short dark hair and tanned complexion.

He smiled at her, catching her gaze momentarily before staring at the fishing lure he held. While she didn't want a man in her life right now, she'd allow herself to look.

Once out of the parking lot, she headed back down Endicott, following the customer who had caught Shea's eye. A lightness had come over her the second she'd walked into O'Leary's and seen Shea. The four years she'd spent in college, she really didn't miss this place, simply because she came home every holiday and for the summers. And really, she wanted to experience something else. To see the world. To know something other than seaside life.

However, she'd been homesick for the last few years.

She tapped her brakes, noting the red light in front of her, but the second it turned green, the truck in front of her squealed its tires and took off into the intersection. Shaking her head, she gave her little car a bit more gas and pushed forward.

Glancing toward the left, she saw the hood of another car just as it slammed into her door, jerking her body. A sharp pain ripped through her head as something smacked her face, and the world faded to black…

Arthur glanced over his shoulder at a grumpy gentleman trying to flirt with Shea. It was pathetic. Horrible. He wanted to step in and perform an intervention. Or ask Shea out for the poor man, but it wasn't his place. Besides, women only served to give him a headache. There were only two things that he desired to do these days.

Work and fish.

Today was all about the latter. Three days of nothing but him, his boat, the ocean, the salty air, a case of beer, a bag of chips, and hopefully a few fish.

Arthur's phone vibrated. He pulled it out and

frowned at a text from an old buddy who worked for a similar outfit in Fool's Gold, Colorado.

Darius: *The trail went cold.*

Arthur: *How cold?*

Darius: *Freezing. But I'll keep looking.*

Arthur: *Thanks.*

The man breezed past him, heading out the door. At least he smiled.

"I've got to get going," a female voice said.

Arthur glanced over his shoulder at the sexy lady who embraced Shea.

His breath left him like a vacuum sucking up crumbs, deflating his lungs. Her eyes were the color of dark chocolate. He'd never seen such richness before. Her long dark hair flowed over her naturally tanned skin. She was the most intoxicating woman he'd ever seen. He blinked, trying desperately to rip his gaze from her, but he couldn't.

He forced himself to turn his attention to some fishing gear. One dead girlfriend and one ex-wife had been more than enough misery for him. He'd sworn off relationships and for the time being, women in general.

"Thirty-two ninety-nine," Shea said. He looked up at her, still reeling from having his socks blown off.

Didn't matter. He had no time for a woman in his life, and if he was going to make time for anything, it would be a dog, but with his schedule at the fire station and his missions with the Aegis Network, he'd have to settle for taking Mrs. Cordelia's lab fishing with him.

He handed Shea thirty-three dollars.

"Need help with the ice?"

"I'm good." He picked up his beer, chips, and lure, then headed out the door, eyeing the sexy woman as she backed her car from the parking spot. He'd seen many good-looking women over the years, but none had made his brain turn to mush.

He sighed, tossing the ice into the cooler. He'd deal with the beer when he got to the marina. Punching the gas harder than necessary, he pulled out onto the street, telling himself he wasn't trying to catch up to the woman in the little car. Why would he do that? What was he going to do? Follow her?

He laughed.

Besides, the light ahead had turned green, and he would not make it through with how far away she was, not even if he had put the pedal to the metal. He tossed his hand over the passenger seat headrest when the sound of tires squealing caught his attention.

Crash!

"Fuck," he muttered, gunning his vehicle, gripping the steering wheel with both hands.

The compact car spun out of control as a four-door sedan smashed into the driver's side. The only thing that stopped the car had been a tree at the corner of the intersection, and the second it hit the wood, the engine ignited.

"Siri, call 9-1-1," he said calmly, though his heart thumped like a jackhammer in his chest. He needed to get the girl out of the car before it exploded.

The sedan raced off down the street. About a half mile before the accident, another truck made a quick U-turn. A light on the dash flashed.

Arthur gave the emergency operator his fire station information along with the location of the accident just as he slammed his vehicle into park.

Mr. Oblivious-to-Flirting quickly stopped, holding out what appeared to be a police badge.

"I'm a fireman," Arthur yelled, grabbing the fire extinguisher from the back of his truck.

"Local policeman. I called it in, and the local

fire trucks are five minutes out. Ten tops. If you've got this, I'm going after that asshole."

"Go." Arthur nodded as he approached the car. Thus far, the fire was contained to the hood, but the car would go up like an IED if it got near the gas line.

He engaged the extinguisher, giving the front of the car a good dousing before racing to the driver's side, which had been mangled and pushed in a good foot.

He cringed, seeing the woman's body slumped over, the seat belt catching her body.

"Ma'am," he called through the broken glass. He reached in, carefully touching the side of her neck in search of a pulse. His fingers immediately found a strong one.

Thank God.

But there was no way he was getting her out of the car through this door. He leaned in. "Ma'am," he repeated as he assessed the situation. Blood dripped down her legs, but the bigger problem was the smell of gas. It pierced through his nostrils. He could taste it in the back of his throat. He glanced to the car's rear and saw the liquid pooling on the pavement.

He doused the front of the car and the leak,

then jogged around to the passenger side, yanking the door open.

Time wasn't on his side.

Story of his fucking life.

The metal screeched and only opened a few inches. He gritted his teeth and yanked again; the door kicked open this time. He leaned in, feeling her legs, making sure that nothing sharp had jabbed into her, which would prevent him from pulling her from the vehicle.

Next, he felt his way up her body and arms, checking for broken bones or any other injuries he could detect from the outside.

A spark on the car's hood flashed, shooting a small flame in the air.

"Ma'am? Can you hear me?"

A faint moan, but that was it.

Another crackle of flames.

He lifted his head, straining to hear sirens, but got nothing.

"I've got to get you out of this car," he said as he undid the seat belt, holding her body upright. He needed to do this with as little movement to her current body position as possible, just in case her injuries were more serious than they appeared.

But that all changed when a trickle of flame moved across the driver's side of the car.

He turned her body, resting her back on his chest, and carefully but quickly pulled her petite body up and over the center console, watching her legs, praying he wasn't inflicting any more damage.

The smoke turned a thick gray-black.

Time was running out.

Leaning over her, he put one arm under her knees and the other circled her back as he lifted her from the seat, stepping backward, cradling her against his chest.

She moaned as he moved away from the car and went across the street to a grassy patch, where he laid her down gently.

Boom!

He covered her body with his as the car exploded, sending debris and tires flying across the road. The few people gathered across the street gasped and screamed but were out of harm's way.

Sirens echoed off in the distance.

Arthur checked the young woman for any external injuries he could treat. He found a few gashes on her legs that he cleaned. One was deep enough that it would need stitches. Her beautiful face was swollen and bruised from the impact of the airbag.

She groaned, her head rolling to the side.

"Ma'am," he said, cupping her face, worrying about a neck injury. "Can you hear me?"

"What?" Her eyelids fluttered open. "What happened?" She tilted her head and groaned.

"Don't move. You were in a car accident."

"Oh…" she whispered.

An ambulance pulled up behind the first fire truck. Two paramedics jumped out.

"Hey, Arthur," a man he recognized from another station said. "We'll take it from here."

Arthur stepped to the side, giving the paramedics room to work, when he heard a woman screaming and running down the road.

"Maren!"

It was the owner of O'Leary's. He jogged toward her, stopping her before she crossed the street.

"You need to give them room," he said, holding on to Shea's arms. "She's conscious, but I don't know the extent of her injuries."

"I have to get ahold of her mother." The woman wrapped her arms around her middle. "I need to be with Maren."

"I can call her mother if you'd like to ride with her to the hospital."

"You don't mind?"

"Sure. Just tell me who to contact."

"Gretchen Cordelia."

He blinked. "That's Maren Cordelia?" His stomach knotted. He'd spent many hours helping Mrs. Cordelia with minor projects around the marina, listening to stories about her daughter and how she wished she'd come home. That the life she chased in New York was not the right life for her. He could understand her wanting her daughter to take over the family business as much as his father had wanted him to be an insurance salesman. Still, after he lost his high school sweetheart and her entire family to a house fire, his fate had been sealed.

She nodded. "What happened?"

"She was T-boned." He left out that it was also a hit-and-run. "Come on." He took her by the elbow and guided her across the street as the first responders lifted Maren onto a gurney. "Hey, guys. This is Shea. She's a friend of Maren's. She'd like to ride with her to the hospital. I'm going to call her mom so she can meet her there."

"Thanks, Arthur," the paramedic said. "Local

police are a couple of minutes out. They're going to want to chat with you."

"I'll wait around." Arthur locked gazes with Maren. "You're going to be okay."

"Thank you," Maren whispered. "Shea?"

"I'm right here." Shea took Maren's hand. "I got you."

Arthur watched as the paramedics lifted Maren into the back of the ambulance. He swallowed, remembering all those he couldn't save, thankful he might have saved her.

3

M aren held the compact makeup mirror, staring at the damage the airbag had done to her face. Her entire body throbbed, especially her thigh, where she'd gotten twenty-five stitches total between the two cuts.

The last thing she remembered before the crash was leaving O'Leary's. The worst part was she struggled to piece together the events after. Shea had filled her in on how a stranger had saved her life.

Now, twenty-four hours later, she still hadn't met the man who had pulled her from the wreckage.

Her mother was finally going to have her way and Maren would come face-to-face with *the* Arthur

Knight, the perfect specimen of a man and a gentleman, according to her mother. She couldn't shut up about him and how wonderful he was with the dog and all the little things that needed to be done around the marina.

"I wish Shea could have returned and gotten us, or even one of your neighbors." Maren knew she should have kept her mouth shut. "I hate to put this man out again, considering he put his life in danger to save mine."

"All the more reason to thank him properly and in person." Her mom tilted her head, lowering her chin as if to scold Maren.

"I agree, but we're asking for another favor just to say thank you. I would have rather done it a different way." And not in front of her mother, who carried a Tupperware container full of cookies because her baked goods solved all the world's problems. But that wasn't the issue. Her mother, bless her kind heart, wanted to control Maren's love life. She wanted Tom out and this Arthur guy in.

That's not how life worked.

"He offered, dear, when he drove me home yesterday."

Maren closed the compact. No amount of makeup could get rid of the dark bruises under her eyes, the cracked lip, or the swollen cheeks. The only way to describe what she looked like was to say she wrestled with an airbag...

And lost.

Ding. Ding.

"Is that your phone?" Maren asked. It was the third freaking time the thing went off and each time, her mom glanced at it as if it were more important than anything else. She was like a teenager who needed to be grounded for rude behavior.

Her mother set the cookies on the hospital bed and reached deep in her purse. "I set different ring-tones for texts, email, Facebook, and Instagram. That is an instant message."

Maren shook her head. Most of her friends couldn't get their parents on social media. She couldn't get her mother off.

"Jefferson is here."

"Jefferson?" Maren questioned.

"You remember Jefferson, don't you?"

"As in the man who used to manage boat sales for us?" She reached into the back of her mind. It had been a few years since Jefferson had worked at the marina, but he didn't stand out in her memory one way or the other.

Her mother pushed her spectacles down on her nose and peered over the rims. "Not us, since you turned your back on the family business, but yes. That Jefferson."

"Mom, why do you have to be like that? I didn't turn my back on anything. I followed what I wanted to do with my life." Or what she thought she wanted to do. Her dreams weren't all that big, but they included cities, travel, and eventually, marriage and family. That all came crashing down a few months ago. Now it was time to shift gears and assess what this older version of herself really wanted out of life.

"Because that's what happened." She tapped away on her cell, smiling like a kid given the keys to a candy store. "You left, making it clear you wanted absolutely nothing to do with the marina. It didn't just break my heart; it broke your father's."

"No, it didn't." She reached out, pushing her mom's hands to her lap. "Daddy wanted me to be my own person. I understand you're upset I didn't come home for any length of time after he died, but I have a career. A life. And you and Dad did talk about selling, which is still an option."

"That's not one I want to entertain. Not while you're—"

Ding. Ding.

Her mother glanced at her cell. "I need to answer Jefferson." She lifted her gaze and smiled. "He's really a sweet man."

"You're dating?"

The corner of her mother's mouth twitched. "One of the reasons I want a partner in the marina. It will give me more time for something like that."

Maren's pulse raced. Not so much because her mother had put herself out there. No. That Maren encouraged. Her mother was a spry sixty-four-year-old woman with many years ahead of her, and Maren wanted her mother to love again. She was too young not to.

"Mom. Selling the marina would give you all the free time and a nice nest egg to work with," Maren said.

Her mother glared over her glasses. "I'd rather have a partner who did the grunt work while I took in the profits."

"All right, but what do you know about this Hudson Nally person?" Maren barely began researching the man when she'd gotten in the car to drive south. Her initial Google search yielded very little, which made her nervous. She figured he'd be all over the internet if he was such a big-time, successful investor.

"He seems like a levelheaded businessman with creative ideas to increase profits."

"I don't want you rushing into anything."

Her mother shook her head. "I'm not stupid, little one. That's why I wanted you to look at things, but ultimately, it's my decision unless you want to come back, and then that's an entirely different conversation."

Leave it to her mother to drop the proverbial hint. Of course, when she found out Maren didn't have a job or a boyfriend, her mother would hit even harder. "Let me take a look at things tomorrow, okay?"

"Oh, honey. Take a few days to heal. That accident was nasty. I hope your job will give you more time off." Her mother dumped her phone in her purse. "I won't be out too late tonight, but don't wait up."

"Wait, what? You're leaving me?" She blinked, staring at her mother. This wasn't like her. Not one bit. Growing up, her mom had been the kind of loving parent who kissed every boo-boo. Drove her to every function. Called every one of her friends' parents to make sure an adult would be supervising when she went to a party. Maren couldn't believe she would up and leave her in her time of need.

"I've got a date. With Jefferson." Her mother smiled. "Wasn't it you who said I should get out more often?"

"But now? Seriously, Mom. You're going to go out with Jefferson and send me home alone with a stranger?" Maren muttered, although she knew how her mother operated, and it was generally underhanded. Even so, her mother's heart was always in the right place.

"And if I told you I had a date, but then canceled it to take you home from the hospital, what would you have done?"

"Taken an Uber. Or called Shea."

Her mother smiled. "But you wanted to thank someone. I'm sure Arthur will be here soon," she said before kissing Maren's cheek. "I'm so glad you're okay and even happier to have you home."

She wrapped her arms around her mom, sucking in a deep breath. "It's good to be back, Mom."

"There's food in the fridge. I won't be late, I promise."

Maren leaned back, fluffing up the pillow.

"Don't you dare make me wait up for you. And no kissy-kissy at the front door."

Her mother laughed shyly. "It's still new. Besides, I haven't kissed a man other than your father in thirty-five years. But if another man's lips need to touch mine, I think I could tolerate Jefferson's."

"Go for it, Mom. Dad would want you to go on with your life."

"That is the truest statement on this planet." Her mother patted the box of cookies. "Arthur is a good man with a kind heart. Give him a chance."

"Mom, I've got to tell you something. Tom and—"

"I know you broke up with Tom." Her mom squeezed her ankle.

Maren opened her mouth, but her mother cupped her cheeks.

"I've known for a while and chose not to say anything because I didn't want to upset you. I might not have liked him that much, but I love you, and all I want is for you to be happy."

Maren sucked in a breath as she released her mother, tucking her knees to her chest. "Did you know I quit my job, too?"

Her mother cocked her head. "That, Tom did not tell me."

"You spoke to Tom?" Bile bubbled up Maren's throat. "When did that happen and you should have told me." That underhanded snake.

"He called me looking to talk to you a few months ago, which is how I found out." She lowered her chin. "He thought you might have come home when you disappeared for a few days."

Maren swallowed her breath. "Well, I just quit my job last week." She lifted the lid off the Tupperware container and pulled out a cookie, breaking it in half. "And don't go getting any ideas about me coming home and taking over the family business." She shoved half the cookie in her mouth, her eyes watering from delight.

Cookies did make things better.

Her mother raised her hands. "I've had ideas since the day you left, but I won't nag you."

"Yeah, right."

"At least not today." Her mother glanced at her phone. "I've got to go. I'll see you tonight."

"I would like to thank Arthur properly, so do you have any ideas other than just thanking him for the ride home?"

"The only thing I know about him is that he's

ex-Air Force, works for the Aegis Network, is a volunteer fireman, he loves fishing, and Shasta follows him around like she's in heat." Her mother fanned her face. "And he's damn good-looking."

Maren watched her mother disappear down the hallway as she drew her good leg up, hugging it, resting her chin on her knee. She closed her eyes and let the details of the sexy man holding a fishing lure enter her brain.

She had to admit, Arthur was hot.

And he'd saved her life. Had he not left O'Leary's when he had, she might not have survived.

In the last twenty-four hours, she'd learned the man who had hit her fled in his vehicle, and the police were still looking for him. They didn't have many leads since the car had been stolen.

She shivered.

No boyfriend. No job.

And now, no car.

Tap. Tap.

She blinked open her eyes, tilting her head toward the door. Swallowing her gasp, she tried not to gawk at the sexy man standing in the doorway. He sported a black T-shirt and a pair of cutoff jean shorts that showed off his tanned, muscular legs.

And freaking flip-flops.

"Arthur?" she questioned, staring into his dark eyes.

"That would be me." He leaned against the doorjamb, folding his arms across his broad chest. "You must be Maren." His smile brightened the room. Her mother was wrong about him being good-looking.

He was fucking gorgeous with his five o'clock shadow, high cheekbones, and those damn intense eyes that captured her gaze and wouldn't let go.

An overwhelming sense of gratitude dripped over her body like a melting piece of chocolate left out in the sun. A sob threatened to bubble up from her gut. "I don't know how to thank you for what you did," she whispered, letting her feet hit the floor.

He shrugged. "Just doing my job."

"You weren't on duty, and you certainly didn't have to come all this way to bring me back to my mother's."

"Not a big deal," he said, taking a few steps into the room. "You look a lot better than when I pulled you from that car."

She smiled, grabbing the side of her cheek, feeling the swollen flesh. "Not by much."

When he grinned, letting out a small laugh, his eyes lightened, becoming a warm, hazelnut color.

"Are you ready?" he asked.

"Just have to let the nurse know my ride is here." She hit the button on the side of her bed.

A long, awkward silence filled the room. He continued to lean against the doorjamb, arms folded across his chest, looking down at the floor, but every once in a while, he glanced up, always catching her staring at him.

She'd never been a shy girl, nor had she ever been at a loss for words. Then again, she'd never nearly died before.

"Will you let me buy you dinner or something? I know I can do nothing to express my gratitude adequately."

He shook his head. "Really, it's not necessary, but thank you," he said in a soft, but distant tone.

She was about to push, but the nurse peeked her head in. "Are you ready to go?"

Maren nodded.

"Good, an orderly can wheel you down to patient discharge."

"Do I have to go out in a wheelchair?" She placed her hand over the bandage on her leg, knowing walking would hurt.

"Hospital rules," the nurse said.

A young man rolled a chair into the room.

Before she lifted her butt off the bed, Arthur was at her side, one hand holding her arm as he practically shoved the poor orderly out of the way to hold the chair steady.

"I can take her down. My truck is right at the discharge doors." He handed her the container of cookies.

"Sorry, hospital policy," the orderly said.

"You can come with us if you must, but I'm pushing her." Arthur stood behind her and gently guided the chair toward the door.

The orderly tossed his hands in the air, shaking his head.

Had Arthur not saved her life, and if she knew him better, she'd be giving him a piece of her mind for being rude. Of course, she was more than curious as to why he'd behaved ungentlemanly.

She glanced over her shoulder with a narrow-eyed stare, catching his gaze.

He shrugged. "Your mother told me to make sure I took good care of you or Shasta wouldn't be able to go fishing with me anymore, and she's my good luck charm."

"So, you're doing this just to spend time with my mother's dog?"

"That, and your mother gives me a discounted rate on my boat slip and storage."

She hadn't meant to laugh, but it was impossible not to when he flashed her a huge, cheeky smile.

The orderly followed them through the hospital corridors and down the elevator until they reached the circle where discharged patients were picked up.

"This is me." Arthur opened the passenger door of the blue pickup she'd seen at O'Leary's the day before. He waved to the security guard on the other end of the circle as he tossed the box of cookies on the center console.

"Did you bribe him to be able to park here?"

Arthur laughed. "He's retired from Delta Force, and I served with him on a few missions. Saved his sorry ass from a burning airplane while in the air." He tucked her legs into the car, being extra careful with her injured one as he gently let it rest on the seat, before slamming the door shut.

She watched him jog around the hood, his short dark hair soaking in the hot Florida sun. He couldn't be any taller than five foot ten, and while he had well-defined muscles, he wasn't bulky. The way the sun stroked his skin sent her hormones into high gear.

Stifle it.

"Please let me buy you dinner," she said as he climbed into the cab and turned the key. "You have to let me repay you somehow."

He tapped the cookie container with his finger. "This is payment enough."

"My mother made those, not me, and trust me, you wouldn't want to eat mine. I didn't inherit her baking skills." She stared at his profile as he drove, one arm resting on the open windowsill, the other drooped over the steering wheel. She remembered seeing him at O'Leary's and noted his serious expression. She remembered blinking her eyes open after the accident and his serious-laden look had been the first thing she'd focused on. In the last half hour, he mostly sported a solemn expression, though when he smiled, something magical happened like when a magician made something disappear and the audience gasped with pleasure.

"I insist," she said.

"If you insist, how about I cook you dinner instead of going out."

She let out a long sigh. "That's not me thanking you. That's you cooking for me."

"You know, the words thank you work better than going out of your way." He turned his head and winked as he pulled into the family home, which was located right next to the marina.

Her heart fluttered like a stupid schoolgirl sharing her peanut butter and jelly sandwich with a boy on the playground. "Not when you save someone's life."

The truck rolled to a stop in front of the garage. She looked at the window next to the front door. Shasta had her nose against the glass, her tail wagging feverishly like she had done when her father would return home from the boathouse.

Her parents had been quite the team in love and in business, but her father took care of most of the significant financial stuff, while her mother was better with people. Maren glanced at Arthur, wondering how close he'd grown to her mother.

"Has my mother ever discussed with you a man named Hudson Nally?" She swallowed. Her mother would have her head if she knew she was discussing her business with anyone, even if it was utterly obvious her mother adored Arthur.

He shook his head. "No. Why?"

"He's offering to invest in the marina so she can

take more time off." She shifted in her seat, getting a better look at Arthur.

"She does work too much." He nodded, lowering his gaze.

"I won't argue with you there, but I don't understand why she wants to bring in an investor, and the fact that this guy approached her makes me pause. There are so many con artists out there taking advantage of people like my mom."

"She's a smart woman."

"Oh, I know that. It's just that she's also very trusting and not the best with money management." She pushed open the truck door and slid from the seat, her legs still weak from the accident.

Gripping the handle, she steadied herself on her good leg.

Arthur looped his arm around her middle. "Lean on me," he said.

She wasn't about to argue, considering how bad the pain was that shot up her thigh when she put her full weight on it.

"Shasta is going to go nuts," he said. "Hopefully she won't jump."

Maren laughed. "That dog is such a spaz."

She looped her arm over Arthur's shoulders,

trying not to let him know how much her fingers appreciated the strength in his shoulders.

Or the soft, subtle skin on his waist as her hand accidentally ended up under his shirt.

When they reached the bottom of the porch stairs, Arthur bent down, tucked his arm under her knees, and scooped her to his chest.

"What the—? What are you doing? Put me down," she protested.

"When we get inside. I don't want Shasta jumping on your leg and opening one of your wounds. Can you unlock the door?"

She dug into her purse, pulled out the set of keys her mother had given her earlier, and unlocked the door. Shasta yelped, her ass and tail wagging so hard she nearly fell over as she raced through the door, running around Arthur, then rising on her hind legs.

"Down," Arthur commanded.

Shasta whined, then ran past them, down the stairs, and did a few circles as if she were chasing her tail, before speeding up the stairs and back into the house, stopping right in front of them by the door.

"Sit," Arthur said.

This time the dog did as she was told.

"Well, I'll be damned. I think that's the first time that dog has done anything anyone has ever asked her."

"Only happens every ten commands."

Shasta barked once, still wagging her tail, following them into the family room.

Maren didn't want to admit that she'd prefer to stay in Arthur's arms as he gently laid her on the sofa in the family room. She half hoped he'd sit down beside her, but instead, Shasta jumped up next to her.

"Get down." Arthur took Shasta's collar and gently eased her from the sofa. "Do you need anything? Water? Food?"

"I'm good, thanks." She fluffed up one of the pillows and shoved it under her knee.

He stood in the middle of the family room, his hands on his hips as he glanced around. "All right, then. I'll let you get some rest."

Shasta grunted as she lay down, dropping her snout to the floor.

"I'll show you out." Maren shifted, trying to stifle a groan.

"You stay put. I'm going to go fishing. I'll check on you when I get back."

Shasta's head popped up, and her tail thumped

the floor the second she heard the word fishing.

"You don't have to do that." Maren patted the dog's head.

"I'm going to be walking right by." He looked from her to the dog.

Shasta looked up at her as if to ask permission.

"You can go." Maren kissed the dog's nose.

Shasta jumped up. If a dog could skip, then that's what she did on her way to the front door.

"Do you want to come?" Arthur asked.

"Thanks, but I think I'm going to try to take a nap."

"Are you sure? I feel bad leaving you here alone."

"I'm exhausted. All I want to do is curl up on this sofa and watch some brainless reality TV."

He laughed. "I'll be back in a couple of hours. Maybe I should leave the dog."

"No. Please, take her. She'll drive me insane."

"All right. Do you have my phone number in case you need something?"

"My mom gave it to me."

"I'll see you shortly," he said.

Maren sat on the sofa for about five minutes after Arthur had left, staring at the ceiling and fanning herself.

The man had made her skin turn to molten lava.

"Come, Shasta." Arthur patted his leg as he strolled down the dock. "Sorry, we had an uneventful trip. The fish just weren't biting."

Shasta trotted alongside him with her tongue hanging out and her tail wagging. She was the happiest, sweetest dog he'd ever met. He wouldn't mind spending the rest of his days with her, instead of people.

He rounded the corner and headed up toward the house.

Gretchen's car wasn't back. He glanced at his watch. It was only eight thirty, but still. It wasn't like her to be out so often in the evening. Granted, the marina had closed at six and she had a good crew.

But she'd left Maren to fend for herself.

He chuckled.

Gretchen had probably assumed he and Maren would spend the evening together. A wave of guilt washed through his veins. However, Maren had made it clear she wanted to nap. What was he supposed to do, sit there and stare at the walls? She was a grown woman and he didn't want to be fixed up with anyone.

Not even someone as strikingly gorgeous as Maren.

Shasta raced off ahead and up the steps, circling in a dance by the front door, which opened seconds later.

"Shit," he mumbled, jogging up the steps. "Down, you damn crazy dog." He got there just in time to catch Maren before she fell over backward as she hobbled on one leg while Shasta jumped up on her hind legs. "Down. Now." He grabbed Shasta's collar. "Come on. Leave Maren alone."

Shasta whined but raced to the sofa, leaping onto the end and curling up in a ball. She yawned, sighed, and plopped her head on her paws.

"Are you okay?" He held her firmly by the hips.

"I'm fine." She grimaced.

"Off the sofa, Shasta." He bent over, looping his arm under Maren's knees, and hoisted her off the floor.

She dug her fingernails into his shoulders. "Oh my God. What are you doing?"

"Getting you off your feet." One of the things Arthur's ex-wife bitched about was his super alpha personality. It drove her crazy. He didn't agree that he was this ultra-controlling man who lived in the dark ages. He didn't dictate what she did. Where she went. Whether or not she worked or stayed home. She was her own person and could make her own decisions in life. However, there were a few things that he did go a little overboard with.

Safety, of any kind, was one of them.

However, Michelle saw it differently. If she broke a glass in the kitchen and he lifted her up and placed her ass on the counter, she took it as he was behaving like an old-fashioned stick in the mud. Maybe he was, but he didn't think wanting to make sure his girl was safe made him a sexist asshole.

"I'm capable of walking."

"I read the discharge papers. You're supposed to take it easy for the next few days." He gave Shasta a good nudge before laying Maren on the edge of the couch. "I'm simply trying to make that easier for you." He took the pillow and gently placed it under her knee before finding Shasta's bone. "There you go, girl. Chew on that for a while and leave Maren alone."

"You're really good with her," Maren said. "My mom hasn't been able to control her since they picked her up from the pound."

"She's a good girl. Just needs a little training. I

wish I had more time to spend with her. I've been a dog lover my entire life. Growing up, we always had at least one, if not two. I've meant to get one since I moved here, but my schedule's been a little crazy." He pointed toward the kitchen. "Can I get you anything to drink? Or make you anything to eat?"

"Water would be nice, and my mother said there was something in the fridge that all I needed to do was heat up." She held up her hand. "If you don't mind, but I don't want to keep you."

"It's no trouble." He turned, making his way into the galley kitchen. He'd been inside the house several times, helping Gretchen out with a few minor fixes and chores. It was a modest, humble four-bedroom home that was in sore need of a few updates. He yanked open the refrigerator and found a container labeled *pasta and shrimp*. He popped it in the microwave, enjoying the garlic scent.

"You can bring it over in the Tupperware. No need to dirty up another dish," she said.

"Sounds good." He rummaged through the drawers until he found a fork. He took down a glass and filled it with water. The microwave dinged. He strolled into the family room and handed it all to Maren. Her beauty still knocked him senseless. "Here you go."

"Thank you."

"My pleasure." He glanced over his shoulder. He should leave. Like now. But instead, he eased his ass into the recliner.

"My mom tells me you're a firefighter and work for some bodyguard-security organization." She dug her fork into a plump shrimp and stuffed it between her kissable lips.

Fuck. What the hell was wrong with him? He couldn't remember the last time a girl had him this twisted in knots. It wasn't as if he didn't have the occasional fling. Hell, he was a man with physical desires and needs. But he didn't want the entanglement and he chose the kind of woman he brought into his bed very carefully. They couldn't be anyone who would get hurt in the process.

That made him a bit of a dick, but at least he was honest.

Maren, from what he knew of her from her mom, wasn't the kind of girl he could have a casual thing with.

"I do."

"How long have you been doing that?"

"Well, I was a fire protection specialist in the Air Force, so firefighting has been my career since I joined the military at age eighteen. But I joined the Aegis Network about six months ago."

"I met Decker Griggs once a few years ago."

Shasta took her bone and settled in at his feet.

"How'd you cross paths with my boss?"

She rolled her eyes. "My dad knew him and my mother decided to play matchmaker. Let's just say it didn't go well."

Arthur burst out laughing.

"I'm not sure why that's so funny."

"Because both Decker and Asher are confirmed bachelors. I'm not sure how your mother managed to get him to agree to go on a date."

Maren waggled her fork. "That's the best part. She didn't. She asked him to come over to discuss a *situation* and thrust me on him. We went out for drinks and stared at each other with not much to say. He came to my dad's funeral. We did get a good laugh out of it and he's a nice man."

"Decker's the best. I love working for him, but he doesn't spend that much time at this office. He's usually down in Orlando."

"That's what he told me. He was only here for a short time, opening up this branch. It meant a lot to my mom that he took the time to fly up here and attend my dad's services."

"That's the kind of guy Decker is." Arthur nodded. He couldn't believe how easy it was to chat with Maren. "Your mom mentioned you're some big financial wiz up in the Big Apple."

Maren laughed. It was a sweet sound that rolled off his ears like melting ice cream over a waffle cone on a hot summer day. "I worked as a chief risk officer. It has nothing to do with financing and everything to do with assessing and managing cyber risk. My job was to look at the data and present a strategic plan to minimize those risks."

Arthur first noticed the use of past tense when Maren referenced her job. He understood that she was here for a few days, maybe a week, to help her mom with a few things before going back to work.

But it sounded like she no longer had a job.

However, it wasn't his place to be nosy, and he wasn't going to dig that deep—at least not tonight.

"Sounds very high-tech," he said. "I have a close friend who is a genius when it comes to cyber shit. He's an IT guru. Darius can hack into any system. It's actually kind of scary."

"He's the guy I'm looking at protecting my company's clients from." She set her bowl on the coffee table.

Headlights from a vehicle pierced through the

window.

His cue to leave.

"I bet that's your mom." He rose and took the dirty dish to the kitchen, rinsed it out, and put it in the dishwasher.

"I can't thank you enough for everything you've done."

"It's my pleasure." He inched closer to the sofa, resting his hand on her shoulder, and squeezed. "I have a few friends down at the police station. I'll keep an eye on the investigation and let you know if they find out anything about the person who hit you."

"I appreciate that." She sat up taller, lifting her chin. "I wish I could see out the window."

"Are you trying to spy on your mother?"

"No," she mumbled. "Okay. Yes."

He chuckled. "Would you like me to do it for you?"

She cringed. "Do you know how many times my mom stood at that very window when I was in high school, waiting to scare off any boy who dared to kiss me goodnight?"

"I imagine all the time." He inched closer to the window. Well, it looks like there will be no kissy-face tonight. Your mother shot that down. Just a hug and now the man in question is heading to his car." Arthur took the four steps to the side door and gripped the handle. He contemplated informing Maren that he'd seen her mom and this guy out before, but again, it was not his place to butt into other people's business. "Good evening, Mrs. Cordelia."

"How many times do I need to tell you to call me Gretchen." She held up her hand, waving it at the dog.

"Shasta, down," Arthur commanded, grabbing the damn dog's collar. "Next time, don't wave. Just hold up your hand."

"You keep telling me that, and I keep waiting for her to knock me over." Gretchen laughed. "So, did you two have a nice evening?"

"I napped. He went fishing," Maren said quickly. It was as if she needed to make sure her mother knew without a doubt he hadn't spent the last three hours in her presence.

He could understand, considering how desperate Gretchen had been for them to meet. "I took Shasta on the boat, hoping it would tire her out, but she's all riled up." He patted the dog's head. "I should head home. If either of you ladies need anything, I'm a phone call away."

"Thanks again for everything." Maren waved from the sofa.

Stepping out on the porch, he glanced toward the sky. His life certainly hadn't been a bed of roses. He had scars on his body.

And his heart.

The things that mattered to him most were his team, his family, and his work. Since his divorce, he didn't believe there was room for anything or anyone else.

Maren tugged at that place in his soul that he'd locked up from the rest of the world and never let out. He never wanted to be in that vulnerable position again. He'd loved and lost in the worst way. And then he'd loved and gotten burned.

Both sucked. Both cut him to the core in different ways.

Neither had stopped him from caring. Or from serving. But they certainly changed his perspective on life.

How could spending a few moments with Maren make him rethink any of it?

He shook his head and jogged down the steps, deciding it was a combination of being tired and the fact his side project had gone completely cold.

Again.

4

Maren set her book in her lap and smiled. "Shea. What on earth are you doing here and with that bag in your hand?"

"I thought you might like the best ice cream in town." Shea climbed the steps on the porch and plopped down in the Adirondack chair, pulling out two to-go dishes. "A fudge sundae for you and strawberry one for me."

"I'm going to get fat hanging around you."

"Once your leg is healed, we can start walking." Shea dug into her treat like it was her last supper. "I'm shocked I'm not three hundred pounds. I actually let myself have some kind of ice cream once a day. But it's the only bad thing I eat. Otherwise, I'm all veggies and good shit."

"You've always been like that. And you exercise like a freak." She lifted the spoon to her mouth and moaned. "Jesus. There is nothing on this earth as good as your family's ice cream."

"That is a true statement." Shea shifted her gaze toward the docks. "I see that Mr. Sexy Firefighter's boat is gone. Did he take crazy dog with him?"

Maren laughed. "He showed up here about an hour after we opened. Shasta went nuts when she heard the rumble of his truck pull in. Damn dog loves him more than me."

"He's around more than you are."

"Now that's just mean," she said. "Especially after I got Shasta as a gift for my parents."

"What do you think of Arthur?" Shea waggled her brows. "Sexy, right?"

"You're as bad as my mother." Maren focused on her treat, shoving a heaping spoonful into her mouth. Her life had been turned upside down. Breaking up with her boyfriend had sent her in a tailspin. It left her with an emptiness in her heart and soul. Nothing made sense anymore, including her career, which is why she'd quit.

But now she had no idea what she wanted.

Being back home made her question her reality. Her life choices.

And Arthur had a different effect. One she hadn't been prepared for.

"It's just a question. I'm simply making girl-friend conversation. Besides, you're the one who confided in me about everything that went down in New York."

Maren groaned. "I was high on painkillers. I didn't know what I was saying."

Shea reached out and took Maren's hand. "We've known each other too long to bullshit each other. You're at a crossroads. I get it. I've been there. Making the decision to come back here wasn't an easy one. Honestly, it made me feel like a failure. But at the end of the day, it's been the best thing I've ever done."

"Are you suggesting I should pack my bags and leave my life in New York?" It's not like Maren hadn't thought about it. But not once had she considered running home to mommy.

Or this marina.

"I can't tell you what to do. But now that you're not tied to New York, you can spend time here. See how you really feel about being back. About the marina." Shea held up her hand. "I had every intention of having my parents sell our family business. It's a hard way to make a living. Trust me, I know. However, I'm so glad that I waited a few months before making any major decisions about that. I love owning it. My parents frustrate the hell out of me. I still have to fight them with changes. But it has been freeing for me. It could be with you too."

"My mother is so hell-bent on having this investor to solve all her problems with me not being here. I agree that if I don't come back, something has to give. But if that's the case, she needs to sell. She's not getting any younger." Maren dropped her empty dish into the bag. "I've been gone too long and I don't know anything about these men she's been talking to."

"I've done some poking around," Shea said. "I'll be honest. I don't have a good feeling about this Hudson Nally guy. Everyone I've talked to says he pushes business owners, hard. Add the fact he's buying Mother's, and that gives me pause."

"It's a prime piece of land. You could do a lot with it."

"Not the point," Shea said. "It's all the other businesses that this man seems to be going after."

Maren's mother waved from the docks as she approached the house. Maren glanced at her watch. "Shit. I'm sorry, but we've got a meeting in fifteen minutes with Nally and his business partner."

Shea stood. "Let me know how it goes and call me if you need anything." She leaned over and kissed Maren's cheek. "I'm always here if you need a friend."

"I appreciate that." Maren watched Shea stroll toward her vehicle, stopping to say hello to her mom for a brief second.

Maren glanced toward the sky as a big puffy white cloud danced across the sun. She had to admit, she missed this. Even if she walked down to the river, or even the ocean, she couldn't capture this in New York. There was nothing like Florida anywhere. And nothing like this little marina. It was a tiny piece of heaven, and she could feel her father glancing down.

"Hey, little one," her mother said. "Did you have a nice visit with Shea?"

"It's so good to see her again," Maren admitted.

"Come on. Let's go inside. We have a few things to discuss before Hudson and his partner get here."

Maren hobbled into the house, taking a seat on the stool in the galley kitchen while her mom bustled about, making tea for the two of them. "Mom, I need you to have an open mind about all of this."

"I was just about to say the same thing to you." Her mother handed her a big mug. Steam floated toward the ceiling. "I know you're concerned, and I hear you on all of it. But you have to understand I can't do this alone anymore and I'm not willing to sell the business. Your father wouldn't have wanted that."

Maren let out a long breath. Her dad wanted the business to stay in the family. She understood that. He had this dream that one day his little girl would be manning the helm. However, right now, she didn't see herself having anything to do with it. She had no idea where her life was going to take her next, and as much as she loved this place, and still viewed it as home, running it overwhelmed her in ways she couldn't explain to herself, much less her mom. "I'm not sure he'd want you to bring on an investor and give them a stake in the business either. Selling it when it's not what I want might be the better option for all of us."

Her mother crinkled her forehead. "Do you have any idea how much that hurts me, little one?"

"That's not my intention. I don't know how to

make us both happy," Maren said. "I will listen to everything they have to say, but we are not signing on the dotted line today."

Her mother lowered her chin. "I'm aware. Your father's lawyer would have my head if I did something that stupid. But I need you to promise me you won't be super combative." Her mother waved her finger. "I know how you get and while I love you for your fierce protectiveness of me, I can't have you putting everyone on edge. Let's listen. Ask appropriate questions. And then call it a day. Okay?"

"I can do that." Maren nodded.

Her mom lifted her cell. "They're at the office."

Maren eased off the stool and followed her mom out of the house and down to the marina office with her heart in her throat. All she wanted for her mom was to enjoy her golden years. Working like a dog to keep the marina going wouldn't provide that. However, she did understand her mom's perspective, thanks in part to Shea.

This was a family legacy.

Her dad had built it from scratch. He'd taken a fishing dock and turned it into a big marina. One that could house a yacht like Rex's. It had become a staple in the community. Their family's name was well respected. She didn't want an investor to tarnish that name.

But suddenly, selling it left a strange taste in her mouth and she wasn't sure how to process it.

"Good afternoon, gentlemen," her mother said. "I'd like to introduce my daughter. This is Maren."

"It's nice to finally meet you. I'm Hudson Nally and this is Michael Santoro."

Maren nodded and smiled.

Both men were dressed in awful button-down Hawaiian style shirts, as if they were trying to fit in, but they most certainly didn't. One wore expensive jeans, the other a pair of dark slacks. Their hair was greased back and something about both men seemed off.

Then again, Maren had always been accused of being guarded when she walked into any business meeting. That her demeanor put clients off.

She squared her shoulders before taking a seat at the small table in the back room.

"Shall we get down to business?" Nally asked.

"By all means," her mom said.

It always amazed Maren how professional her mother could be in any given situation. It was like she was two different people sometimes. The sweet, nice older lady who appeared to be the person anyone could take advantage of.

Until you put her in a room full of salesmen.

But today, her mom was a little too eager.

"Here is the contract." Michael passed around a document that Maren thought was too thin.

She took a copy and immediately dived in. The numbers appeared fair and reasonable. They had valued the business at about twelve percent under the market value. Something she would have to change.

Their return wasn't outrageous.

But it was their level of involvement that threw her for a loop. Not only did they want a stake, but they wanted to be hands on. Not necessarily a bad thing. But she hadn't realized how much these men had planned on participating in the marina. What the hell did they know? She thought the concept was to give money so that more people could be hired to do the heavy lifting and to expand, giving her mother the freedom to retire.

She glanced at her mom, who tapped her pencil on the table.

"May I ask a few questions?" Maren said.

"Please." Hudson folded his hands on the table.

"I've heard you're investing in other businesses.

Are you going to have this level of involvement in those?" She held up her hand. "I'm only asking because this contract states that you will be bringing in managers to oversee the day-to-day. I feel that my mom and I would be better suited to find those people, especially when my mom is ready to retire and she'll still have controlling interest."

"When we invest, we view it as a partnership," Nally said with a smile. "One or two of our people sprinkled in will only bring a new perspective, ensuring that the business flourishes." He tapped the contract. "If you flip to page three, you'll see that your mom will have the power to make the majority of the decisions. But if we're going to invest, we need to ensure our money is going to the right places. It's a win-win."

Maren wasn't sure if she saw it that way. But contracts were meant to be negotiated. "I'm not sure I like how quickly you want to make these changes in staff." She flipped through the document. "Or some of these other changes you're proposing."

"This marina isn't living up to its potential," Michael said. "Our job as investors is to make improvements. That's what our money is going toward. It's all for the greater good and I believe your mother sees that, don't you?"

"Lord knows we can use some updating," her mom said.

"Good. We're all in agreement, then." Nally handed her mom a pen. "All we need now is a signature."

Maren opened her mouth but didn't have to say a single word because her mother did it for her, thank God.

"Before I sign anything, I need to have my attorney look this over," her mom said. "There are a few sticking points I might want to change, and then we might have a deal."

"Mrs. Cordelia," Hudson said softly. "I don't mean to play hardball with someone as nice as you. But our funds are limited and there are a dozen businesses up and down this shoreline hammering to do business with us. This deal will go away in a day or two." He stood. "I'd really like to be partners with you. I believe we're a good fit. I hope you'll sign." He stuffed his copy into his briefcase and he and Michael shuffled out the door.

"I didn't like that last statement, Mom," Maren said. "Business deals don't go away that quickly, unless they're fishy."

"Or they're playing the game." Her mother pointed toward the back window. "Look. Arthur is pulling in with our dog. Why don't you go see if he'd like to have dinner with us. I'll fax over the contract to Daddy's lawyer. I'm sure he'll have one or two changes he'd like to make and we'll go back with a counteroffer."

"I'm not sure I want to counter," Maren said.

"Unless you're willing to come back and run this place, it's not your decision to make." Her mom waved her hand. "Now go ask Arthur if he's hungry."

"Yes, Mother." Maren let out a long breath. There was no arguing with her mom when she got like this. She might as well go find Arthur. Maybe he'd finally let her thank him properly.

5

Arthur tossed a nice-sized snapper into the cooler. All in all, it had been a good day on the ocean. The sun shone bright. The waves were light. And the fish were biting. The only problem was, he couldn't get Maren, among other things, off his mind.

It had been five years since his short-lived marriage ended, and in that time, Arthur hadn't met a woman who fascinated him to the point that she'd crept her way into his dreams.

When he woke up this morning, the only thing he could think about was the vision of Maren dancing in his mind like sugar plums.

The dream hadn't been anything spectacular as

far as dreams went. He'd taken Maren and the dog out on his boat. There was light conversation, hand-holding, but then out of the blue, he'd pulled her into his arms and pressed his lips firmly against hers in a sizzling scorcher of a kiss.

That had been what jarred him from his sleep. The last time he'd felt a stirring that deep had been with his ex-wife. Michelle was a magnetic woman. Deeply passionate about her work as a fundraiser for underprivileged children. She had a big heart and he adored that about her.

But Michelle struggled to forgive and forget. That woman could hold a grudge longer than anyone he knew. The second her feathers got ruffled, for whatever reason, that was it. She didn't care if she was right or wrong. It didn't matter. If she was pissed, she'd stay that way for days. Weeks even. Once he was deployed for three weeks. They fought the day he left. He thought for sure she would have calmed down by the time he returned. He came bearing gifts and a heartfelt apology.

She wouldn't even listen.

That had been the beginning of the end. Love and marriage shouldn't be that hard. Of course, Michelle always tossed Sarah in his face.

He blinked, reliving the haunting memories of the house that had been burned to the ground, killing everyone inside, changing his life.

He pulled his wallet out of his back pocket and reached for the faded picture. Nineteen years had passed since he had kissed Sarah on the front porch of her parents' home for the very last time. Had he known, he might not have left that weekend with his buddies for a fishing trip.

Running his finger over the top of her head in the picture, he allowed the memories to flood his mind like a kaleidoscope of the best and worst year of his life.

"I'm going to find who killed you and your family and I'm going to make them pay. I promise," he whispered. He kissed the image and then put it back in his wallet.

Shasta whined, bringing his mind to the present and the dark-haired woman who made him question his desire to stifle anything other than casual sex. Shit. The second that thought hit his brain, he cringed. He wasn't an asshole for not wanting a long-term relationship. But putting that idea out in the universe suddenly seemed inappropriate.

"Let's get you home, big girl." He fired up the

engines and pushed the throttles. The bow rose out of the water before planning off. He navigated through the channel and slowed when he hit the no-wake zone.

God, he loved days like these. Birds chirped in the sky. Other boaters waved as they passed with their favorite country music song blaring. All this gave Arthur the chance to mask the pain he'd been carrying in his heart for the last eighteen years.

The afternoon sun beat down on his face as he pulled the boat into the marina. Shasta stood on the bow, her tail wagging feverishly, always making Arthur smile. The life of a dog was simple, and Arthur had strived to make his life as unpretentious as possible, devoting his time and energy to work and fishing.

His buddies often busted his balls about the way he lived. They called him a minimalist. Not that anyone but Rex had the financial freedom to live however they wanted. But Arthur took it to the extreme as he currently lived in a one-bedroom apartment that was barely furnished.

"Yo, Arthur!" Rex waved from the yacht he kept at the end of the dock where Arthur's boat was moored. "Hey, Shasta, you're a good girl. I bet you are."

Shasta barked twice. She lowered her head to her front paws and her butt moved back and forth with her tail. It looked as if she wanted to jump off the boat and swim right to Rex.

"Stay, Shasta," Arthur said, just in case.

Rex had grown up with a silver spoon in his mouth. He could afford things that Arthur and the rest of the guys couldn't even imagine, but there was an uneasiness to Rex that no amount of money could satisfy. And honestly, Rex didn't use money to feed his inner beast. Sure, he had a yacht. A couple of cars.

"Catch anything?" Rex asked.

"A few snappers. And one nice size Mai."

"Were you planning on freezing it? Or would you like to share? Buddy, Duncan, and Kent were just about to order a pizza."

Arthur pushed the throttle to neutral, letting the boat drift into the slip. "Sounds like I'm coming aboard. Just let me bring Shasta back up to the main house while you assholes come get the fish off my boat."

"Why is it that we're always doing the heavy lifting?" Rex asked.

"Because I was team leader in the Air Force, I'm your boss at the station, and I have—"

"Shut the fuck up." Rex laughed.

Shasta yelped a few times as she jumped from the boat to the dock, her toenails skidding across the wood planks.

"Relax, girl," Arthur said, but Shasta took off toward the boathouse. That's when Arthur saw Maren hobbling down the dock and her dog racing toward her. All Arthur could picture was Shasta jumping on Maren, hurting the cuts on her leg or knocking her off-balance and sending her into the ocean.

"Shasta! Come." Arthur jumped from the boat, tossing Rex the line, keeping an eye on Maren and the dog that almost never listened. He jogged down the dock. "Shasta!"

Maren held on to one of the posts as if to brace for impact. She raised a hand.

Thankfully, Shasta slid to a stop a few feet away.

"Sit," Maren said, holding up her hand.

But the dog did the complete opposite and bolted.

Shit.

Arthur got to Maren and the dog just as Shasta rose up on her hind legs.

"Oh no, you don't." Arthur reached out, grabbing the dog around her shoulders, pulling her to his chest, and scratching her belly. "No jumping on pretty ladies. It's not nice."

Shasta whimpered as he set her paws down on the dock.

"Thank you. She jumped on me three times this morning, once landing right on my stitches." Maren patted the section of her thigh covered with a gauze pad. "But I have to admit, she's a lot calmer and listens better than she used to. My mom says that's all thanks to you."

"She's a good dog." Arthur patted Shasta's head. "How are you feeling this afternoon?"

"Like my car nearly blew up." She laughed. "And I look like someone used my face as a punching bag." She cupped her cheek.

"It's not that bad, and you look better than you did yesterday," he said. "What are you doing down here? You should be resting."

"I was in the marina, talking with my mom and the potential investor, and I saw you coming in. My mom thought I should invite you up for dinner." She spoke clearly, but the pace at which the words flew out of her mouth made him wonder if she had a little nervous energy.

The thought pulled at the corners of his mouth.

"Your mom thought? Or you thought?" He arched a brow. The need for clarification gave him a good sucker punch.

"My mom suggested it, right before she informed me she had a date. So, this is her way of shoving the two of us together again." Her smile made his breath hitch. "But I still haven't thanked you properly, so I'm game if you are."

"You've thanked me plenty." He glanced over his shoulder. His buddies stood on the stern of Rex's yacht, doing their best to act as if they weren't staring. "I'm supposed to have dinner with those lug nuts." When he turned to face her, he looked past her, off into the parking lot where he saw two men getting into a dark sedan.

One of the men looked a little too familiar.

He took a step around her and squinted. "Is that the investor? What was his name?"

"Hudson Nally."

"Which one is Nally? Who is the other guy?" Arthur pointed toward the car with his heart hammering in his throat.

"Nally is the one about to get into the driver's side and the other guy's name is Michael Santoro. Why?"

Neither name rang a bell, but the Santoro guy looked a little too much like Richie Hernandez, who was the muscle for Alberto Ferro, one of the largest drug traffickers in all of Texas. Only what would he be doing in Florida using an assumed name?

"I'm sure it's nothing, but has your mother signed anything yet?" The last thing he wanted to do was spook Maren or her mother. Not until he found out for sure, and from this distance, he couldn't be one hundred percent sure he was looking at Richie.

"Not yet. Why are you asking about that?" Maren's fingers curled around his biceps, shocking his body with sparks flying from his head to his toes. It surprised him that he had such a visceral reaction to her touch. Maybe it was because of the quick clash between the past and the present. Whatever it was, this wasn't the time or place.

"Hang on." He pried her fingers off his arm and took off in a full-out jog toward the car, cell phone in hand.

The two men had climbed inside the vehicle, but before they moved out of the parking lot, he'd been able to snap a picture of the license plate.

Arthur: *Find out whatever you can on this plate, specifically if there is a connection to Ferro.*

Darius: *Got it! But I want more information.*

Arthur: *I think I might have saw Hernandez. My eyes could have been playing tricks on me, but who knows. Anyway, let me know what you find out.*

Darius: *Anything for you.*

Arthur turned, glancing between the marina's main building and Maren, who limped in his direction with a scowl and a dog at her side.

"Mind telling me what that was all about?" She stopped a few feet in front of him with her hands on her hips and narrowed eyes.

He minded all right, but only because he didn't want to scare her if he was wrong.

On the other hand, maybe she should be frightened.

"I honestly don't know, but don't let your mother sign anything with those people until I can do some more digging," he said sternly, which he wished he could have taken back.

She folded her arms across her chest. "How do you know them? I also want a specific reason why I need to keep my mom from signing. Not just because you're asking a lot of us to go on your blanket statement, but because this is none of your business."

By the way her glare burned his skin, he better give her some answers. He contemplated for a couple of seconds, taking into consideration all the different scenarios and stories he could spin.

"The man you say is Santoro looks an awful lot like a man wanted for arson in a different state. I want to make sure I'm wrong."

"Arson?" Both her brows shot up. "You're joking, right?"

"No, ma'am, I'm not." He opted to leave out the fact that many federal agencies were watching Ferro and his organization, trying to nail the bastard on anything. "It's probably not the same guy, but better safe than sorry."

Maren wrapped her arms around her middle. "I have to admit, I got a bad vibe from them. They remind me of a snake oil salesman. I know the type. They say the right things. Have all the right answers. And honestly, I have my reservations."

He pressed his hand on the small of her back, his thumb gently rubbing near her spine. "I'll walk you up to the house while you tell me why."

She cocked her head. He didn't know if her

reaction was from the way he touched her or the situation.

He went with the latter.

"They assumed they would walk out of here with a deal. Kudos to my mom for not needing me to step in and tell them we needed time to look over the contracts. Discuss it. And have our lawyer take a look."

"Your mom's a smart woman," he said. "Is the deal a good one?" He glanced toward the waterfront. Rex stood on the back of his boat, tossing his hands to the sides.

Arthur gave him nod, indicating he'd be back down. He needed to stay close to the marina and keep a watchful eye on Maren and her mother.

Without having to share the same space as Maren because he might do something stupid like kiss her.

"It's not horrible, but it has some problems. And it concerns me that they are investing in a place like Mother's, too." Maren's leg obviously bothered her as she continued to limp, leaning against him.

He curled his fingers around her hip, helping her to take some of the pressure off. "Did they leave you with the paperwork?"

She nodded. "What bothers me the most is my mom told them she needed to discuss this with me, so when we told them we needed more time to look everything over and had a few other questions, they mentioned how they had limited funds and had other businesses in the area beating down their doors, so tomorrow the offer might not be there. I get that tactic. I've seen it a million times in business, but it seemed over the top in this particular situation."

"How did you leave things?" he asked as they stood at the bottom of the porch steps. Placing his hand on her other hip, he turned her to face him.

"That we'd discuss it and get back to them after we had a chance to go over everything."

He watched her lips move, painfully aware that his hands were on her body and his mouth wanted to devour hers, which was completely inappropriate considering the topic. Taking a step back, he dropped his hands. "Do you mind if I take a look at the offer?"

She glanced up at the house as the front door swung open and Shasta raced inside.

"Hello, Arthur," Gretchen said with a bright smile. "Care to come in for a drink? Some dinner? I've got lasagna in the oven."

"Thanks, but I'm having dinner with Rex and some of the guys tonight."

"Oh, well, that's too bad. Maybe another time?"

"Absolutely," he said a little too enthusiastically.

"Mom, can you get the paperwork with Mr. Nally's offer? Arthur has some concerns, and I think it would be good to have another set of eyes on it."

"I suppose we can do that," Gretchen said with a scowl. "But I called Jefferson, and he believes it's a good deal."

Maren looked between him and her mother, and he suspected she contemplated telling her mother his thoughts about who Santoro might be.

He gave his head the slightest of shakes, hoping she caught the movement.

Maren squeezed his biceps, her warm hand burning his skin with fiery passion. "It can't hurt us to have Arthur look at the offer. You trust him and since we're both on the fence, maybe he can add some insight. I get you trust Jefferson and we've known him a long time. No offense, Mom, but Arthur doesn't have any skin in this game. Jefferson has a bit of an ulterior motive. He wants to free up your time. I'm not saying that's a bad thing. It's just reality."

"All right. I'll go get the papers they left behind."

He kept his focus anywhere but on the woman standing in front of him with her fingers electrifying his skin.

"Looks like I owe you another big thank you," she said.

He shook his head. The pull she had over him made his insides melt, but it tore his heart in two.

"No. Seriously. I know it's not much of a gesture, but please, let me take you out to dinner or something else. Whatever you enjoy doing. It would mean a lot to me." Her dark eyes pleaded with him like sad puppy eyes that no decent human being could possibly say no to.

But he would have to.

"I've only got another day off, and then I'm back on duty at the station and who knows what the Aegis Network will throw in my direction." His skin cooled the second she dropped her hand.

"Oh. I see." The hurt in her tone sucker punched his gut, but it was the hint of sadness that radiated from her hickory-rich-as-the-earth's-soil eyes that made his heart beat a little faster.

"I really do appreciate the offer, and if I had more time—"

"Here you go, Arthur." Gretchen appeared, handing him a thin folder. "Sure you don't want to have a drink with us?"

"How about tomorrow evening when I return the papers?" He smiled at Maren, hoping she'd smile back.

Well, a slight smile was better than nothing.

"Perfect," Gretchen said.

"Good night, Arthur." Maren turned and hobbled up the stairs, leaving him standing at the bottom, feeling like the utter idiot he was.

Dumbass. How hard is it to have one fucking dinner with a woman? It wasn't like she was after him to get married or anything.

The moon danced across the dark sky, casting a white glow over the water as Maren stared out into the marina at the boat with Arthur and his buddies, which was all lit up. Faint music echoed in the night. She could only see silhouettes of the men aboard, but she knew exactly which one was Arthur.

The one sitting at the table, nursing a longneck, with papers in his other hand.

Maren wrestled with the corkscrew until the cork popped off and the smell of dry pears filled her senses. Nothing like a good dry white wine.

Normally, she wasn't the type of person to drink alone, but between being jobless, nearly dying, and her mother getting more dating action than her, Maren figured a few glasses were just what the doctor ordered.

She put the bottle on ice and brought it out to the front porch.

Growing up, she never thought it was weird living at the marina with her house across the parking lot, overlooking the long docks that stretched out into the Intracoastal Waterway, housing everything from pleasure boats, to fishing boats, to million-dollar yachts. She hated to admit it, but it felt good to be home, even if only temporarily.

Though she knew without a doubt she did not want to return to New York City. She'd never been cut out for that lifestyle. However, she had no idea what she wanted to do or where she wanted to go. The last five years of her life had been about Tom. Every decision she made had been based on what Tom might think or want.

The days of putting a man before herself were over.

Laughter rippled across the water, stealing her attention, reminding her of Arthur and his stubbornness. She hadn't really taken offense to his refusal to allow her the slightest gesture of gratitude, but more, it piqued her curiosity as to why he was so opposed to having dinner.

Maybe he had a girlfriend?

Maren nixed that idea quickly. If he had one, she was sure he wouldn't be spending one of his last night's off work with his buddies. Besides, he probably would have told her when she asked for the millionth time.

Maybe he was gay?

She laughed out loud. Well, anything was possible.

Regardless, she was going to think of a way to repay him.

Fishing stuff!

Quickly, she pulled out her phone. "Hey Siri, call Shea O'Leary."

"Calling Shea O'Leary."

Got to love modern technology.

"Hello?" Shea's voice bellowed from the speaker. "Maren? Everything okay?"

"Yeah, I'm fine. Listen, I was wondering if you could help me out with a gift for Arthur." Maren swirled her wine, staring at the liquid as the moon's rays glistened through the glass.

"I don't really know him all that well."

"Does he shop at your store often?"

"Often enough, why?"

She took a small sip of the crisp, cool wine. "Since he won't let me buy him dinner, I thought I'd get him a bunch of fishing gear. Tackle. Poles. Whatever he generally buys and maybe a few hundred dollars in bait that he can use at his leisure."

"I can help you with that. Can you swing by sometime tomorrow?"

"Sure."

"Hey, babe, are you ready?" A muffled male voice filtered through the phone speaker.

"One second, okay, Rusty?" Shea asked. "Sorry, I've got a date with that guy from the shop the other day. You remember, the angry one."

"Yeah, and he tried to chase down the asshole who hit me. Please thank him for me, and I'd like to do something for him as well."

"No way, sister. He's all mine."

Maren laughed. "I'll see you tomorrow, and you better fill me in on all the details from tonight."

"Come around lunchtime and we can sit down for a bit."

"Sounds like a plan." Maren tapped the phone before setting it down on the table. The faint hum of a motorboat engine tickled her ears. She loved the sounds of the water, whether it be the lapping of waves against the shore, birds overhead, or even the annoying owl that lived in the live oak covered in Spanish moss in the backyard.

The ripples from a boat danced under the moonlight, but the small vessel had no lights on.

Idiots.

She stood, taking the first few steps down the porch when she saw a flame fly from the boat, heading toward the dock right where the gas pumps were located.

"No!" She dropped her glass and it shattered at her feet as she raced down the steps, ignoring the pain in her thigh as well as the sharp tear in the soft part of her arch.

The flame landed about twenty feet from the gas, but whatever the flame was attached to rolled down the dock, dangerously close.

As she barreled down the dock, Arthur and his

men leaped into action, taking what must have been fire extinguishers, and began dousing the flames that kicked up as the wood dock ignited.

Another firebomb flew through the air, this time landing on a boat, which immediately caught fire, sending thick smoke and orange flames into the sky.

"Take my boat and go after them," Arthur shouted.

Maren ripped off her shirt and wrapped her hand in the fabric before smashing the glass to the emergency fire hose at the base of the dock.

The crackle of flames grew stronger as the flames tore through the boat, getting way too close to others. She didn't know much about fires, but she knew enough that if they didn't contain this one, her entire marina, and the men on the dock, would go up in one colossal explosion of epic proportion.

She quickly hooked up the hose and tried cranking the wheel to get the water flowing, to no avail.

"Get back," Arthur ordered as he shoved her aside, taking the hose in his one hand and turning the wheel effortlessly in the other. He looked her up and down before yanking off his shirt as the water flowed from the hose. "Put this on, you're half-naked."

She didn't argue, tugging his shirt over her head.

"I'll get another extinguisher from the—"

"Just stay away from the docks, got it?" He lowered his chin, glaring.

"I can help."

"You want to help? Go to the street and wait for the first responders to get here and bring them down. I already called it in."

If someone could shoot daggers from their eyes, it would be in the expression on Arthur's face with his narrowed stare and furrowed brow.

"Listen." She took a step forward.

"I told you to stay back." He pressed her hand against his chest. "I can't be worried about you and do my job. Now just go."

"But—"

"Maren, just do as you are fucking told and go wait for the fire trucks while I try to save your goddamn marina."

She gasped, then snapped her mouth shut. Heat erupted from her toes, scalding her skin right to her forehead.

Arthur turned and ran down the dock with the hose. Had the flames for the boat not just flicked higher in the sky, she would have marched herself down the docks and given him a piece of her mind.

Instead, she shuffled up to the parking lot, her thigh aching and her foot throbbing. Sirens blared in the distance.

She glanced over her shoulder. Arthur and his men worked to contain the fire.

Well, at least she knew for sure that this time a simple thank you would be all he deserved.

6

A rthur sat on the steps leading up to the front porch of Maren's home. Luckily, the fire had been contained to part of the main dock and two boats. God only knows what would have happened if he and his crew had not been there.

"No news on the hit-and-run?" Arthur asked Rusty, the off-duty police officer who had witnessed Maren's accident.

"Nothing on the guy driving the car, but the forensic team says the tire marks from the other car are not from braking, but from peeling out."

Arthur snapped his head up. "As in they could have been waiting for the right time to race through the intersection?"

"That's the theory we're going with."

"Have you ever heard of Alberto Ferro?"

Rusty tilted his head. "He's got a place in Miami and rumor has it, he's expanding his business up the coast. Why?"

"I think one of his thugs might be responsible for tonight's fire."

"Which means you think he's behind Maren's hit-and-run."

"Exactly," Arthur said.

"I'll look into it."

"I appreciate that." Arthur glanced over his shoulder as the front door screeched open. Maren and her friend Shea stood at the door, hugging one another.

"I'll see you tomorrow," Maren said to her friend, then glared at him as she slammed the door shut.

He guessed he deserved that.

"She finally got ahold of her mother." Shea breezed past him before slipping her arm around Rusty's waist. "She's about an hour away."

"Thanks," Arthur said, rubbing his temples. "How's Maren?"

"Pissed at you," Shea said with a sprinkle of sarcasm and a heaping cup of annoyance. "Not to mention she's got a cut on her foot that I think should have had stitches."

"I assume the paramedics patched her up?"

"They did. She's a tough cookie."

"I imagine she is," Arthur said, wondering if she was going to open the door in a few minutes when he knocked on it.

"I'll be in touch," Rusty said.

The couple headed toward the parking lot. Never in a million years would he have expected those two to walk off arm in arm.

But life was full of unexpected events.

Like the rush of emotion he'd felt over the idea of Maren being in harm's way and anywhere near that fire. He resisted the urge to take out the picture of Sarah. The thought that any of this could be related to Sarah and her family's deaths disturbed him to the core. But what made his insides twist in pain was the thought that history might repeat itself.

It wasn't about people dying in fires. He could only save so many, a reality in his career he had to reconcile. Nor was it about his past, even though that affected him with every fire he battled.

This was about Maren.

A woman he'd just met.

A woman who had wormed her way into his daily thoughts and his nightly dreams.

A woman he wanted more than he'd wanted anything in a long time.

He stood, sucking in a deep breath, and made his way to the front door where he tapped his knuckle three times.

Shasta barked. He could see her sitting in front of the door, wagging her tail. Maren stood at the breakfast bar in the kitchen, doing her best to ignore him.

He banged again.

This time Shasta raced to Maren, groaned, then ran back to the door, jumping up.

"Come on, Maren, open the door."

When she didn't turn around, Arthur took a chance and twisted the knob.

Unlocked.

"Down girl," he whispered, patting the dog's head.

Maren looked over her shoulder. "I already said thank you. I don't think I need to say it again."

"No. But I need to apologize." He made his way to the kitchen island and sat down on the stool beside her, pulling out his wallet and setting it on the counter. "I only snapped because I didn't want anything bad to happen to you."

"That's no excuse for the way you behaved."

"You're right." He opened his wallet and pulled out the picture of him and Sarah taken before the junior prom with both sets of parents. "But maybe this will help you understand." He pushed the picture across the countertop with a shaky hand. Other than his parents, his two sisters, and Darius, he hadn't spoken to anyone about Sarah, her family, or their murder in years.

Maren cocked her head, holding the picture between her long, slender fingers. "Are you married? Is this your wife? Girlfriend?"

"She was my high school sweetheart, and she and her family died in a house fire when I was seventeen." The words rolled off his tongue a little too easily. He wanted to feel the pain and guilt for having feelings for another woman. He wanted to wallow in self-pity and loathing.

But all he could do was see this beautiful woman, full of life, sitting next him, making him feel things he had no intention of ever having in his life again. "They were murdered."

"Oh. My. God." Maren dropped the picture. "I'm sorry. I had no idea."

"You had no way of knowing. It's not something I talk about, but I couldn't let you go on the dock and risk something tragic happening to you. I..." He what? He cared? He valued human life and did his best to protect it, but when he'd watched her rip off her shirt to open the emergency fire hose, something primal erupted in his heart.

Something he hadn't ever felt before, not with Sarah and not with his ex. He didn't welcome the sensation.

"I care very much about your mother and after pulling you from a burning car, well, let's just say I care about you, too." There. He'd said it. He rubbed his shaky hands on his thighs, suddenly aware he had no shirt on. "I'm sorry I yelled at you, but I'm not sorry for keeping you off that dock."

"Thank you for that." Her fingers traced the edges of the picture. "Who murdered them and why?"

He rested his arms on the counter, dropping his forehead to his hands and swallowing his breath. Maybe telling her what happened would help make her understand just how bad these men were.

"To make a very long story short, her father owned a restaurant and he took money from an investor who turned out to be a criminal and used the business to launder his money. When Sarah's father found out, he went to turn the bastard in, only Ferro got to him first, setting the family home on fire. No one got out alive." Arthur clenched his eyes closed, fighting the tears that threatened. He didn't cry for himself anymore, but for the fact he hadn't been able to bring the family any justice.

Much less peace.

"Is that why you became a firefighter? Joined the Air Force?"

He rolled his head to the side, catching her caring gaze. "Yes." He wanted desperately to fight the pull Maren had over him. To deny how comfortable he felt in her presence. To destroy any emotion he had. But no matter what he did, he couldn't push her from his mind.

"And now you think this guy that Nally brought is somehow related to the people who murdered the love of your life?"

For a short year, Sarah had been his world. He'd been seventeen and not even close to being a man yet, something his adult mind constantly challenged with every short-lived relationship he'd had over the years.

"I really don't know, but since the murderer of Sarah and her family has never been brought to justice, I can't let go of the uncanny similarities between this Santoro guy and someone I know to be associated with Sarah's death. Add in your accident and tonight's fire, and my instincts are on high alert."

She leaned back on the stool, resting her hand on his bare back, rubbing up and down. Her skin tingled against his, sending signals to the rest of his body. He thought he should stifle it, but he honestly didn't want to, and that scared him.

"I'm sorry about what happened to your girlfriend and her family."

"Thank you," he whispered. "I'm sorry I was an asshole."

"Yeah, you were." She patted his shoulder, giving it an intense squeeze.

He should sit taller and ask for a shirt, but instead, he kept his head on the counter, enjoying her tender touch, wondering what it would feel like to kiss her lips, neck, collarbone... hell, every inch of her.

"Tell your mother not to take this deal."

"I don't know. While I don't like their pushy tactics, this might be just what my mother needs."

"Are you kidding me? After what I just told you?" Sitting up, he turned his body to face her, resting a hand on her good knee. "That fire tonight was intentional, and I believe it was meant to scare your mom into taking the deal."

"Oh, come on. That's not the first time some stupid teenagers raced by and—"

"Tried to blow the place up?" he interrupted, drilling his point home.

"We've had vandals before."

He arched a brow.

"Seriously, what would they gain in starting a fire? If they destroyed the marina, there'd be nothing to invest in."

"If these people are who I think they are, this place would be the perfect business for them to run drugs and launder money, especially if they had to rebuild."

She laughed. "I'm sorry, but that's absurd."

Hopping off the stool, he started to pace, scratching the back of his head. "Then explain the hit-and-run." He stopped and held up his hand. "And before you try, Rusty informed me that the tire marks on the road were not of the car trying to brake, but of a car accelerating, intentionally barreling through that intersection."

"What? How can they tell?"

"The difference between how a tire increases during—"

"It was a rhetorical question." She stared at him, her wide eyes flickering with fear and confusion.

"You need to shut this deal down. Now." He held her gaze, doing his best to keep his emotions in check. The combination of anger and desire could be a bad mix where he was concerned, and the last thing he wanted with Maren was angry sex.

"I don't know, even though we don't like their pushy tactics, it's a perfect—"

"Are you even listening to me?" He reached out and grabbed her by the shoulders, holding tight. "These are some seriously bad people who do whatever it takes to get what they want."

"Let go of me."

He let out a long breath, dropping his hands, but he clenched his fists. "Someone may have tried to kill you, and for all we know, this fire could have been for the same reason."

"That's crazy. Why would they want to kill me?"

"That's an easy one. It would make taking advantage of your mother so much easier. Get to the daughter, who seems to be standing between them and the marina, so they can get what they want." He shifted forward, his nose only inches from hers. "Tell them unequivocally, no."

"Don't tell me what to do. I hate that more than anything."

He tossed his hands wide and stared at the ceiling. "Would you for one second stop and really hear what I'm saying?"

"It's kind of hard when you turn into a controlling asshole." She planted her hands on her hips and jutted her chin out. "I'm sorry about what happened to your girlfriend, but that's not what is going on here, and I think you need to find a way to let go of—"

He covered her mouth with his hand. "Don't go there. The only thing I'm holding on to right now is wanting justice for an innocent family and making sure it doesn't happen to someone else I care about." He breathed in deeply, letting it out slowly as he uncovered her mouth, her shocked eyes glowering at him.

She raised her hand and poked her index finger in the center of his chest. "Don't you ever touch me like that again. And care about me? You don't even know me."

He grabbed her hand and placed it over his heart. "I know enough that I want to know more.

Hell, I want to know everything, but I'm not going to get a chance if I'm pulling your dead body from the bottom of the Intracoastal." He didn't give her a chance to respond as he meshed his mouth with hers.

He knew he sounded over the top and crazy regarding his wanting to explore something with her, as well as his theory of Ferro's goon wanting to kill or at least maim her. He'd gone from wanting to avoid her at every turn, to never wanting to ever leave her side. Of course, part of that was due to the fact he knew without a doubt, whoever Nally and Santoro turned out to be, they worked for Ferro.

And Ferro would stop at nothing to get what he wanted.

Arthur gripped her hips as he parted her lips with his tongue in search of hers. She greeted him tentatively as her fists came down on his shoulders. He expected her to shove him away, but instead, her fingers dug into his skin and glided over his shoulders and down the middle of his back.

As the kiss became a dance between wild animals, his hands roamed her body, starting under her shirt, feeling the curves of her back, enjoying how she arched as if he'd found that one spot that tickled. He rubbed his palms over her firm ass before cupping the back of her thighs and hoisting her off her feet, setting her butt on the counter and pressing himself between her legs.

Wanting to feel skin on skin, he curled his fingers over the bottom of her shirt. He pried his lips from hers as he yanked the fabric over her head. Her chest heaved up and down with every raspy breath.

He caught her gaze and smiled at the lust he'd put in her molten eyes. His fingers found the hooks on the back of her bra and, with little effort, unfastened the garment, enjoying how her pupils dilated as her eyes widened with a combination of shock and delight.

Kissing her neck, he let the straps fall off her shoulders. If he were being a gentleman, he'd ask her if she wanted him to stop or if it was too soon. Especially since they hadn't even had dinner or a date, much less spent any real time together. But here he was, kissing his way down her collarbone, his index finger pushing the lacy fabric down, exposing the perfect round nipple.

He should be slowing down, taking his time, but that thought left his brain the moment he sucked her tight nub into his mouth, devouring her like a wild beast who didn't know the art of lovemaking.

The way her hands threaded through his hair encouraged him to explore more, kissing his way down her stomach. He pulled at the top of her jeans with his teeth, glancing up at her.

He groaned as she bit down on her lower lip and pressed her fingers against the button on her pants, easily undoing it. He swallowed, watching her fingers lower the zipper, revealing lacy white panties.

"Bedroom," he managed to ground out as he stood, cupping her ass and wrapping her legs around his waist.

"Up the stairs, second door on the right." She wiggled against him, smiling, knowing exactly what she was doing to him.

"You're going to pay for that."

"God, I hope so."

He strolled to the steps, doing his best not to stagger as he climbed them, holding her body tight so her skin touched his.

"This is crazy," he whispered as he kicked open the door. "You're home for how long?" He laid her on the bed as gently as he could without ripping their bodies apart.

"A week. Maybe two."

He kneeled between her legs, shimmying her shorts and panties over her hips, almost hoping that his better judgment would kick in before she lay gloriously naked under the moonlight filtering in through the window. "So, this is just a one-night stand kind of thing."

She rose up on her elbows, hands covering her breasts. "Can we please not classify this and get on with it before I remember I'm really ticked off at you? Not to mention I don't even know…"

He yanked her shorts to her ankles, nearly pulling her off the bed.

"Whoa."

"You told me to get on with it." As he undid the button and zipper on his shorts, staring down at what had to be the most gorgeous woman in the world with her dark complexion, silky skin, and brazen eyes, his hands trembled, and his heart pounded in his chest. He shouldn't be doing this, and he was about to take a step back when she batted his hands away and jerked his clothes to his ankles.

Choking on his breath, he tried to collect his gentleman qualities when she grabbed him, holding him in her soft hands as her pink tongue flicked out over the tip of him.

"Jesus," he muttered, gently pushing her hair aside, his chest rising and falling with his raspy, desperate breath as he stared at her. She caressed and teased him to the point his vision blurred and his thighs grew weak. It took all his control not to press her head further onto him, though she certainly didn't need any encouragement as he watched himself disappear inside her hot mouth.

He tugged at her hair, yanking her head back. "Come here," he commanded, bringing her to a standing position. He took her chin between his forefinger and thumb, tilting her head. "You ready to scream with pure pleasure?" Lifting her leg, placing her foot on the bed, he cupped her womanhood, groaning at the wetness lining his palm.

"I don't scream or beg. Just for the record."

"I think I can change that." Gliding his finger over her opening, circling her tender lips, he did his best to contain his primal desire to take her with force.

Her hands gripped his shoulders while he at first slowly stroked her insides, feeling her tighten around his fingers. The way her body responded to his touch brought the blood in his veins to a boil.

As he slipped two more fingers into her wet folds, her moans turned to desperate guttural groans. Her hips rolled against his hand. He bent over, sucking on one of her nipples and more hot, creamy liquid poured over his hand.

"Oh. My. God," she whispered in a deep, husky voice.

He sucked harder and fingered faster, his need to make her orgasm so strong, it was all that mattered.

"Yes!" Her hips jerked.

He released her nipple, kissing the underswell of her breasts. "Come on, Maren, come for me." Curling his fingers inside her, he stroked her a few more times before pulling his hand out, rubbing her swollen nub, then starting the movement all over again.

"Oh… Oh… God." Her moan echoed through the room.

The power that came with making a woman orgasm with just his hand had always been intoxicating, but with Maren?

He lost all power and succumbed to her desires and wishes.

"Do you want it like this?" He kissed his way up her neck. "Tell me what you want, Maren."

Her fingers dug into his shoulders, her body rocking back and forth. "Like this. Now," she cried out, cupping his face.

She clenched down over his fingers and squeezed her legs together.

"Oh.... Oh... Arthur!" She tossed her head back and forth.

A sense of pride filled his gut. "I told you I'd make you scream. Now, let's see about making you beg."

She cocked her head, smiling wickedly. When her lips brushed his, he knew he was in for the ride of a lifetime. "You're the one who is going to be begging."

"Oh, really." He arched a brow, intrigued and totally turned on by the banter. "And exactly how do you plan on making me beg?"

Her tongue parted his lips, swirling inside his mouth with a fiery passion that sent his body into a panic that he'd never get enough of.

Just as he wrapped his hands around her luscious body, she pushed away, climbing on the bed, maneuvering herself against the headboard and propped up some pillows. "You have to stay there."

"What?"

She smiled, raising one hand to her breast, pinching and tugging at her nipple. "You can't move." Next, she glided a hand down her firm stomach, rubbing her forefinger against herself, spreading her legs wide.

"Jesus Christ," he mumbled, raising his hand to himself.

She waggled a finger at him. "You can't touch yourself either."

He dropped his hand to his side. "Tease me like that and I'm bound to climb on this bed and take you."

"I'll let you know when that would be acceptable."

"Acceptable." His voice cracked like a pimply-faced teenager as he watched her fingers dance over her womanhood.

Her soft moans tickled his skin. His breath hitched as he watched her bring herself pleasure.

"You've got maybe three more minutes before I'm on top of you." He looked around the room. "Shit. I left my wallet downstairs."

"Why do you need that?"

"Because that's where I have a condom."

She smiled, bringing her fingers to her lips, sucking them into her mouth slowly.

He growled.

"No worries. I have one."

"Yeah. Where?" he asked right after he swallowed his breath.

"My overnight kit on the dresser behind you."

"Keep doing that." He waved his hand in the air as he stepped backward, careful not to take his eyes off her, admiring the glistening of her body and learning from her how she touched herself. Not that he'd use it since the second he covered himself, he'd be all in and nothing would be able to stop him from taking her with raw and unabated force.

Goosebumps lined his skin and his body shivered. The way she stared at him as he ripped open the foil package with his teeth and swathed himself with the condom sent a warm tingle to all his nerve endings.

"Get on all fours." He knelt on the foot of the bed. "This isn't going to be pretty or last very long, but I promise you're going to have another orgasm." God, he hoped he'd be able to make good on his promise.

"Demanding, aren't you?"

"Are you going to do as I ask?"

She smiled, rolling over to all fours, positioning herself with her ass in the air, looking over her shoulder. For a second, he stopped breathing and his heart stopped beating. This should not be how one made love to a woman for the first time, especially when he cared about her.

And Arthur honestly cared about Maren.

Yet here he was, taking her like a sex-starved animal.

He grabbed her hips, pulling her to him, entering her with one hard, commanding stroke. Rocking back on his heels, he lifted her to him, giving his one hand access to her breasts, while his other hand rubbed her hard nub, making her moan, rocking her body against his.

Gritting his teeth, he did what he could to maintain control as their bodies intertwined in a primitive dance meant to call on all the sexual gods.

Her arms reached over her head, circling around his neck, her head resting on his shoulder.

He continued to thrust, completely losing himself in her. "Please," he begged. "For me, Maren."

She rolled her head, kissing his cheek, lowering a hand and covering his as she pressed it harder against herself, creating a friction so intense, his body ignited in a hot, electric flame.

"Oh, yes," she said softly as she quivered at his

touch, her climax spilling out over him in a hot wave.

He could no longer contain himself as he pumped inside her, growling as he let his release spill out. "Jesus, Maren," he whispered. "You make me crazy."

"And I made you beg."

He let out a small laugh as he continued to slowly stroke the side of her before shoving her stomach down on the bed and collapsing on top of her, totally spent. The actual act of sex didn't last very long, but the effects continued to linger while he tried to catch his breath.

"You begged," she cooed, her hands reaching around him, squeezing his thighs.

He chuckled. "I did and you came again."

"And again."

He rolled to his side, pulling her body against his. "Give me ten minutes and I could do it again."

She popped her head up. "Did you hear that?"

"Hear what..." He looked out the window. "You mean tires against gravel?"

"Yeah. I think my mother is home."

7

Maren stared into Arthur's eyes as the reality of the situation sank in. "She's really home."

"Shit." He jumped out of bed so quickly he tripped over the tangled bedspread and fell to the floor.

She covered her mouth to stifle the fit of laughter that erupted from her lips.

"Not funny," he mumbled as he hiked up his pants and looked around the room. "Where's my shirt?"

"You took it off me downstairs, remember?"

"Right."

"Just get down there before my mother gets to the porch. I'll be down shortly."

"What do I say about where you are?" He glanced between her and the window, his eyes wide with a confused glow.

"That I'm changing out of my dirty clothes."

"That works." He turned, heading for the door, but paused. "I'm sorry that ended as abruptly as it did. I'm usually the kind of guy who enjoys a good cuddle afterward. Maybe next time."

She swallowed as he disappeared, the sound of his feet hitting the floorboards beat with her pounding heart.

What the hell had she just let happen?

One minute she's arguing with a control freak, the next she's got her mouth where it doesn't belong.

Her ex had been a power-driven prick in business, and he turned out to be that way in their relationship, though she rarely put up with it. She'd been a free spirit most of her life, doing what she wanted, when she wanted, and not worrying too much about what others thought. That strong personality was what helped her get the hell out of this sleepy little seaside town.

But that drive and determination that went with it facilitated the demise of a career she ended up resenting and a boyfriend she didn't like, bringing her back home and into the arms of a stranger who gave her the most incredible burning desire to take a chance on him.

And her hometown.

No!

The idea that Arthur thought there could be a next time sent a heat wave across her skin.

This had to go down as the dumbest, most reckless thing she'd ever done next to the day she and a few friends climbed onto one of the customers' million-dollar yachts and partied like rock stars her senior year of high school.

That didn't end well, and she suspected whatever this thing with Arthur was wouldn't end well either.

Besides, he was still pining after a dead girl.

Hearing the front door slam shut, she slinked out of bed. Her thigh and foot throbbed, while her body, drenched in the aftereffects of sex, tingled with unadulterated passion.

"Maren, honey?" her mother's voice bellowed up the stairs.

"I'm coming." Maren sucked in a deep breath as she ran her fingers through her hair, making sure it was smooth and didn't look like she'd just gotten out of bed. She took tentative steps, telling herself it was because her wounds hurt, but the reality was she didn't want to face the man downstairs.

Her mother greeted her at the bottom of the steps with open arms. "Come here, little one."

Maren rolled her eyes. God, sometimes she hated when her mother called her that, and the last thing she needed was her mother hugging her so tight it took her breath away. As she eased into her mother's arms, she stole a glance at Arthur, who leaned against the kitchen counter next to an older gentleman whom she recognized as Jefferson.

Arthur's lips were drawn into a tight, tense line until he caught her gaze, then he cracked a slight smile.

She couldn't help it, she smiled back.

"Are you sure you're okay?" Her mother cupped her face, staring deep into her eyes.

"I'm fine. Really."

"Thank God Arthur and his friends were still here."

She nodded as her mother took her by the hand and led her through the open family room into the kitchen. "We owe him a world of gratitude again."

"We sure do," her mother said. "You remember Jefferson, don't you, dear?"

Jefferson had aged a little with a few extra

pounds around the middle and salt-and-pepper hair, but he was still a handsome man.

"Good to see you again, though I'm sorry about the circumstances." Jefferson extended his hand.

"It's been a crazy few days," she admitted, taking a seat on the bar stool next to Arthur, trying not to make it obvious that her knee was touching his thigh.

"I don't like the idea of you two girls here alone," Jefferson said, scratching the back of his head. "But my mother is eighty-nine, and I can't leave her alone too long."

"They won't be alone." Arthur rested his arm on the counter behind her back and while he didn't touch her, her skin bristled with the heat he generated. "I will be staying here." His voice had that same commanding tone he'd had on the docks earlier.

On the one hand, she couldn't stand it. She knew he came from a place of caring, but it didn't change the fact she didn't respond well to it.

"That won't be necessary." She jerked her knee away and that didn't go unnoticed by him.

"I think it's a good idea. It would make me feel better," Jefferson said.

"I hate to put you out like that, Arthur," her mother said.

"It's not a problem. Even when I'm at the station, one of my team members can be here." Arthur slid his hand across the countertop, his thumb gently touching her back.

She shifted.

"I'm going to call that friend about fixing and updating the security system," Jefferson said, pulling out a stool for her mother. "Do the police have any leads? Any theories?"

Creating better security around the marina certainly was something Maren could get on board with, but having a personal bodyguard wasn't part of that package.

"Probably just some stupid kids drinking too much and doing something on a dare," Maren said, ignoring Arthur's scowl.

"That would be one hell of a dangerous dare," Jefferson said.

"And not what happened." Arthur rested his forearms on the kitchen counter. "I have a buddy looking into a possible connection—"

She kicked his shin.

His body jerked as he reached down, rubbing his leg. "Jesus, Maren, that was uncalled for."

"I would say so," her mother said with a stern voice. "I apologize for my daughter's behavior."

"I'm not a small child, so don't go saying sorry for me." Maren poked Arthur in the biceps. "And there is no need for you to go spewing your theories, making my mother worry even more." She arched a brow.

"Ignorance is not bliss in this case, and it certainly won't keep either of you safe." He jabbed her shoulder with his index finger.

"Are you two done acting like adolescents? Because I really want to hear what Arthur has to say about the events of this evening," Jefferson said with an exasperated sigh.

"As I was saying." Arthur glowered at her, almost daring her to try to shut him up again. "I'm concerned that Maren's accident is related to tonight's fire."

Her mother gasped, covering her mouth. "Oh my God. Someone hit her car on purpose?"

Maren wanted to point out this was exactly why she didn't want to tell her mother, but she bit her tongue.

"The police have some evidence that points them in that direction and earlier tonight, when Nally left, I thought I recognized his associate as a man who was involved in an arson case in another state."

"What exactly are you saying, son?" Jefferson rested his hand on her mother's shoulder.

"I believe the men who want to invest in this place would be using it to launder money as well as run drugs out of the marina."

"Holy shit," her mother whispered.

"It's a theory." Maren knew the facts, and they told her that Arthur could be right, but he made it sound like it was the only possibility and that just pissed her off.

A phone vibrating on the counter made everyone in the room jump.

"That's me." Arthur took the phone and held it up. "I've got a text from my buddy Darius… Shit." He turned the phone so everyone could see. "Theory, huh?" His stare narrowed. "Nally's associate, what was his name, Santoro? Is actually Richie Hernandez, a known criminal, working for the drug cartel run by a guy by the name of Ferro." Arthur pointed to his phone. "That is fact. Not theory and you two ladies aren't going anywhere alone until that asshole is behind bars."

"Oh, God." Her mother leaned into Jefferson. "Someone tried to kill my baby?"

Maren swallowed, staring at the images on Arthur's phone. She couldn't deny the reality staring her in the face.

"Why would he do that?" Jefferson asked, both hands on her mother's shoulders, massaging gently.

"I suspect right now it's a scare tactic, to push you to let them invest or sell to them outright, but I don't put murder past these people." Arthur turned, holding the phone to his ear.

"Who are you calling?" Maren resented the tremble vibrating in her throat and the shaking of her hands. She'd been afraid a time or two walking in New York City alone at night, but seeing those images and knowing… no, accepting that Arthur was right disturbed her to the core.

"Rusty, to give him all this information and then a few of my buddies so they can help with security. I'm not letting anything happen to you or your mom on my watch."

"This is just horrible," her mother said, moving to the stool next to Maren. "I'm sorry I ever gave those men the time of day."

"It's not your fault." Maren pulled her mother in for a hug, holding her a little tighter, wondering if she hadn't come back to town, how this all would have played out. She shivered.

"I'm sorry. I hate that I have to leave," Jefferson said, standing behind her mother. "I'll see what I can do about getting more help with my mom."

"Thanks, Jefferson. I really appreciate it," her mom said.

"I'll call you in the morning." Jefferson leaned over and kissed her mother's temple. "Arthur, walk me to my car?"

"Sure thing. I've got to get my go bag anyway."

Maren eyed Arthur as the front door clicked closed.

"Not to change the subject or anything," her mother said, leaning forward, clutching Maren's hands.

"Please, if it's a more pleasant topic than money laundering and drug cartels, do tell."

Her mother tilted her head. "Why is your bra on the floor? And why did Arthur just try to kick it under the chair?" She pointed toward the small wingback chair between the kitchen and great room.

Heat rose to her cheeks.

Her mother smiled. "I knew you two would like each other."

8

Arthur sat on the front steps, sipping his coffee and rubbing the back of Shasta's ears. If he'd gotten three hours of sleep, it would have been a miracle. But a hot shower and a little caffeine would be all that he needed to stay alert. Besides, having most of the crew on the marina grounds would give him a chance to power nap if he needed.

Nally had called first thing and Gretchen had given him the bad news, which he didn't really accept, constantly pushing her to reconsider. The conversation ended with Nally saying he'd stop by at some point today to discuss the matter.

Something Arthur didn't want to happen at all,

but Rusty thought it might help them get something on him, or get a positive ID on Santoro being Hernandez, because as Rusty put it, "Just because they look like they could be the same person, doesn't mean they are." Not to mention, Santoro had a valid driver's license and social security number.

Didn't mean he was who he pretended to be, but it made it more difficult to call him out.

The door behind him rattled. Shasta yelped and her tail thumped back and forth.

"Good morning," Maren said, sitting down, keeping Shasta between them. Last night, she'd gone up to bed before he'd even come back inside from getting his bag. He texted her, asking if they could talk. She responded with 'in the morning.' "How was the sofa?"

"Much better than a cargo hold of a C-130, thank you."

Shasta rested her snout on Maren's leg, and Arthur refused to stop scratching the dog's head. This was about as close to Maren as he figured she'd allow.

"I'm afraid," she said, staring off toward the Intracoastal. "And there isn't much that scares me."

"I'm honestly fearful of these people myself. Over the years, I've seen the devastation they've left behind as they destroy lives and tear apart families."

"Besides fishing, is chasing after your late girl-friend's killers how you pass the time?"

He swallowed. So, she thought he was still holding on to the memory of Sarah in such a way that it hadn't let him move forward. Sometimes he could be such an asshole. "When she first died, we had no idea they'd been murdered or that her family had been in business with Ferro. It took about a year before all that unraveled and made the news."

"And you've made it your life's journey to bring her killers to justice. I get it."

He shook his head. "No, you don't." He pulled out his phone and brought up the dreaded Face-book app. The only pictures of him on the internet were on his ex-wife's page, which he'd often asked her not to post his picture, and that was probably another of the many reasons their marriage only lasted a little over two years.

"I don't need to see pictures of your late girl-friend and her family. Really, Arthur, I understand. I can't imagine—"

"Would you just be quiet for one minute?"

"When you stop being an asshole, maybe." She let out a long breath. "Listen. I can't stand being told what to do or how to act. It makes me nuts. Compound it with a man who acts like I'm not capable of taking care of myself, and it makes—"

"Seriously? That's what you think I've been doing?"

"Um, yeah?" She jerked her head. "Anyone ever tell you that you can be a controlling prick?"

He chuckled. "Once or twice. And I'm sorry. But has anyone ever told you that you're stubborn, pigheaded, and don't listen?"

"Once or twice," she mumbled.

"I honestly don't mean to be so controlling, except maybe when I'm trying to save your life or make a point." He found the picture from his wedding day and practically shoved his phone in her face.

"You're married?" She grabbed the phone, gawking between the screen and him. "Wow. Before, I just thought you were kind of sad with your heart wrapped up in your late girlfriend, but now all I see is a two-timing jerk and a—"

"Oh my God." He smacked his head. "Seriously, stop talking and let me finish." He snagged the phone and returned to his ex's profile page, holding a new image up. "I'm divorced and she's already remarried. You really need to stop jumping to conclusions about me, which is funny because that's what you accused me of doing with the scumbags that are hell-bent on causing you bodily harm."

She snapped her mouth closed, staring at him. He took the opportunity to continue talking while the cat still held her tongue.

"I loved Sarah as much as any pimply-faced seventeen-year-old boy could. I probably cried every day over her death for a good year, and her death did push me into my profession, though I had always wanted to be a fireman since I was a little kid." He took a quick breath. "When it came out what had happened, I turned to someone I'd met through a mutual friend. He was in the Army and now works for an outfit like the Aegis Network. We've been trying to find whatever we can to give to the authorities to bring down Ferro. I want to help bring a sense of peace to her grandparents, aunts, uncles, cousins, and other families affected by the shitty-ass things Ferro has done, but it's not something that has completely taken over my life until they showed up here, messing with people I care about."

Her gaze never wavered from his as she sat quietly.

He blinked.

"Are you done?" she asked.

"Yeah, I'm done."

"Can I ask a question without you getting mad at me?"

"I can't promise that," he said.

"Fair enough." She nodded. "Why'd you get divorced? Was it because of your pursuit for justice?"

"That's one of a million reasons my ex-wife gave for finally putting us both out of our misery. Mostly, it's hard being in the military and being married, and she wanted me to retire. I wasn't ready at the time. And frankly, I don't take kindly to ultimatums. She thought she could change me, and I thought she'd accept that I'm not the kind of guy who wants to go to parties every weekend. And she really wanted me to give up fishing."

"Well, that right there is way too much to ask." Maren smiled.

He let out a small laugh.

"Look. I'm sorry I jumped to conclusions

about your late girlfriend and even your ex-wife. I'm also sorry that I got in your face last night, arguing with you about those men and their intentions. It's your delivery. You can be aggressive. It reminds me of someone I used to be with and I won't ever get involved with someone like that again."

He arched a brow. "Do you regret being with me last night?"

"I regret getting caught by my mother."

"Almost getting caught," he corrected.

"No. We got caught. My mother saw you kick my bra under the chair. Real smooth, Arthur."

He closed his eyes for a moment. "And here, your mother thought I was such a gentleman."

Maren rested her hand on Arthur's forearm. "I'm really scared about what is happening, but I'm also a little terrified of you."

"Me? Why?" That wasn't what he expected to hear.

"I tossed and turned half the night, thinking about texting you to come upstairs."

"That wouldn't have been a good idea."

"Especially with my mother in the next room, but I wouldn't have kicked you out and that bothers me."

"Not something a man wants to hear from the woman he just had sex with."

"I don't know how to reconcile what I'm feeling with what is now honest-to-goodness fear for mine and my mother's life. I find myself relying on you, but you can be so controlling and I just got out of a relationship with a control freak who cheated on me, so I don't want a repeat of history."

Ouch. That hurt.

He nodded. "I've been gun-shy since my divorce when it comes to women, so to be totally up front, I'm a little freaked out myself by how quickly we ended up in bed." He reached his hand out, pushing her hair off her shoulder and gliding his hand across the back of her neck. "But I don't for one second regret it, and I plan on it happening again."

She opened her mouth, but he kept her from saying anything by slipping his tongue between her lips and swirling it with hers in a promissory dance of pleasure.

Shasta barked, sitting up, forcing the kiss to end long before Arthur wanted it to.

"What is it, girl?" He patted the dog's head as the sound of loose gravel being crunched by tires stole his attention.

A limo rolled to a stop in the middle of the parking lot.

"Know any boaters that would show up in a ride like that?" he asked. "Besides Rex?"

"We've had a few."

He kept his hand on the back of Maren's neck, rubbing his thumb in a circle at the base of her head.

She stretched her leg out as if to stand.

He squeezed her shoulder. "You're staying right here."

"You've got to stop being so controlling if you ever want to get back in my bed."

He chuckled. "Being protective is my nature. It's not controlling who you are. And we'll be together again, regardless."

"You're impossible."

"Yep."

The driver stepped from the vehicle and opened the rear door.

Arthur found himself holding his breath, waiting to see who would appear from the back seat.

He didn't have to wait long as a tall, broad man with dark features appeared. Arthur's lungs deflated in a rush as if someone had poked them with a sharp object.

"Fuck," he muttered.

"What?" Maren asked.

"That's him."

"Him who?"

Arthur turned to look at Maren. "That's Ferro."

9

Maren stared at the man standing in a light-green designer dress shirt, designer slacks, neatly pressed, and pointed boots that looked like the skin of a reptile.

"Would he recognize you?" she asked in a whisper.

"I don't think so." Arthur took her hand, helping her up. "I met him once when I was a kid visiting Sarah at the restaurant. I was scrawny with a face full of pimples. Not to mention I was two inches shorter. I was a late bloomer."

"Well, you've certainly bloomed real nice."

He laughed while she squeezed his hand so hard she thought it might hurt.

"What do you think he wants?"

"Put Shasta in the house and let's find out."

"Don't you think we need a watch dog?"

"Because licking a man to death is always the way to deal with criminals." He opened the door, letting the dog race inside. "Besides, I don't want to be distracted or worried about Shasta while talking to Ferro."

She sucked in a deep breath as she followed Arthur down the porch steps, trying desperately to calm her racing heart. She'd met her fair share of corrupt businessmen who were willing to sell out their own mother in order to make a buck.

But none of them would have ever killed anyone, at least not intentionally.

"Sorry to disturb you," Ferro said as he sauntered across the broken parking lot. "Is Mrs. Gretchen Cordelia available?"

"I'm her daughter, Maren. How can we help you?"

"Maren Cordelia." Ferro reached out and took her hand in his. "It's a pleasure to meet you. I've heard a lot about you."

"Excuse me? From who?" Maren's heart pumped harder as her stomach rolled.

"That's not important." He raised her hand, pressing his slimy lips against her skin.

She shivered, eyeing the five men stepping from the limo, all carrying weapons.

"Arthur, Arthur, Arthur." Ferro shook his head. "What am I going to do with you?"

Arthur reached out in front of her, pushing her behind him. "I could wager a guess as to what you think you're going to do to me, but that's not going to happen because you're going to leave. Now."

"I'm not going anywhere." Ferro puffed out his chest, nodding his head to one of his men. "Let's go find the old lady."

"You leave my mother alone." Maren tried to charge forward, but Arthur grabbed her by the shoulders as one of Ferro's men shoved a gun in her face.

"Tell your buddies to stand down, or we will kill you right here." A tall man with a sinister smile stepped to within two feet of Arthur and pressed a gun to his temple.

"I need to signal them." Arthur didn't flinch.

Maren swallowed a sob. Her insides rattled like an asteroid crashing into the earth's surface.

"Go right ahead, then let's go find the lovely Mrs. Cordelia."

Maren watched as Arthur raised his arm in the

air, making a whirlybird motion, then pursed his lips, making three different whistling noises.

Two men emerged from different places, all holding their hands up in the air.

"Everyone to the marina office," Ferro said.

Maren leaned into Arthur as he wrapped a protective arm around her middle, almost acting as if no one had pointed a gun at her or him. She wanted to feel safe in his arms, but that was hard to do when almost a half dozen men, heavily armed, walked next to them.

"Mom," she whispered as her mother stepped from the office door.

Arthur's body tensed. "Go inside, Gretchen."

"What's going on? Who are these... Oh, my."

"This isn't going to end the way you think," Arthur said with a dark tone.

Ferro laughed. "I might have walked away from pushing this deal had I not known you were hanging around. You've been a little thorn in my side for years with you and your buddies trying to stir up trouble for me."

Maren moved her legs faster, wanting to get to her mother. Her face had grown pale, and she gripped the doorknob, frozen in place with her mouth gaping open.

Arthur continued to hold on to her until they reached the office, where she bolted to her mom. "Are you okay?"

"No, dear, I'm not. Those men have guns," Gretchen said.

"I know." Maren hugged her mother, drawing her back into the office. She glanced over her shoulder. Only Arthur, Ferro, and two men entered the building. The other men must be doing something with Arthur's men.

She shuddered. Her skin grew cold.

Those men had nothing to do with this situation and didn't have to be here.

The bell over the entryway chimed.

Jefferson stepped through the door.

Her mother raced over to him. "Jefferson!" She flung her arms around him.

He, on the other hand, coolly held her at a distance.

"Nice of you to finally join the party," Ferro said.

"Fuck," Arthur muttered.

Maren reached for her mother as she stepped back, her face white as porcelain.

"Jefferson?" her mother questioned.

Maren narrowed her eyes, mentally stabbing

Jefferson in the heart. "You told him everything we told you last night."

"Your mother should have just signed the papers. Had she, none of this would be happening now," Jefferson said.

"How could you be part of this?" her mother asked as she held on tight to Maren. "Why?"

"Money. Why else." Jefferson shrugged.

"But we gave you an excellent retirement package," her mother said, her words laced with shock.

Jefferson laughed. "Your husband pushed me to retire long before I was ready."

"You set me up," her mother's tone infused with rage. "You bastard."

"Mrs. Cordelia, please sit down." Ferro pulled out the chair behind the desk. "Let's sign the bill of sale."

"I'm not signing anything," Gretchen said.

One of Ferro's men lifted his rifle, pressing it against Maren's temple, the metal hot against her skin. Tears pooled in the corners of her eyes.

"You won't get away with any of this," Maren said.

"Oh, we will. And you're going to help us." Ferro leaned against the desk, setting a stack of papers in front of her mother along with a pen.

"These make me a fifty-one-percent partner of the marina. We're going to make great business associates."

"And then what? You let us walk out of here?" Arthur asked as he moved closer, his hand gripping hers in a tender but protective touch.

"Oh, the two ladies do." Ferro tapped the papers.

"With everything we know, you're going to let us live, just like that?" Maren's pulse raged. Her body shook. She shouldn't have asked such a stupid question.

Ferro waved his hand in the air. "If either of you lovely ladies utter a single word to anyone about what is going on, one of you will die a very slow and painful death while the other watches." Ferro pushed himself from the desk, waltzing over toward Maren. He snagged a fistful of hair and yanked her head back.

"Let her go," Arthur said with a menacing growl.

One of Ferro's men jabbed Arthur in the gut with the butt of his weapon.

Maren tried to swallow, but her head had been pulled back so far she couldn't.

Ferro kissed her neck. "I think Mother should watch me fuck her—"

"Get your hands off her." Arthur lunged forward.

Crack!

The man with the gun used it to smash the side of Arthur's face. He dropped to the floor, blood spurting from the side of his mouth. He groaned as he got to his knees.

Ferro released her, and she raced around the desk to stand by her mother, who sobbed uncontrollably.

One of Ferro's men hoisted Arthur to his feet, cuffing his hands behind his back with some wiry thing that reminded her of a twist tie used to close the turkey cooking bag.

"Take him out to the boat and get rid of him and his two friends."

"Two friends? There were four here last night," Jefferson said.

Ferro grabbed Maren again, taking out a knife, pressing the blade against her neck. Gripping his forearm, she tried not to move as the jagged edge tore at her skin. "Where are the other two men?"

"On the roof," Arthur said behind a tight jaw,

staring at her, his eyes glowing with a combination of rage and sadness.

Ferro pointed to one of his men. "Find them and bring them down to the boat."

The blade twisted against her skin and warm liquid drizzled down her neck.

"Stop hurting her. I'll tell my men to surrender." His eyes swirled into an array of darkness. He looked at her as if he were apologizing.

She closed her eyes. She might not have known Arthur very well, but she knew him well enough to know if he'd given up, then there was no hope at all.

10

Arthur knew Rex had been on the roof the entire time and with the window open, Arthur had to believe Rex had heard everything.

Now all he had to do was get out of the zip tie restraints and beat the shit out of the asshole that had made him bleed.

Then there was Ferro. It would take a fucking miracle to keep Arthur from taking the knife Ferro held to Maren's neck and jabbing it into Ferro's heart a half dozen times, watching his face as his life slowly faded into the abyss.

That asshole had taken away one woman he'd loved.

No fucking way would Arthur allow history to repeat itself.

The goon that had cuffed him now gripped his biceps and yanked him toward the door.

"Where are you taking me?"

"To your demise," Ferro said.

Arthur didn't fight it. He hated leaving Maren and her mother in the office, but right now, he had no choice.

Ferro wouldn't bat an eyelash at ordering one of his men to put a bullet in Arthur's head and that wouldn't help Maren one bit.

Besides, Arthur didn't feel like dying today.

Once outside, he scanned the area.

Fuck.

Kent, Buddy, and Duncan were on their knees, hands in the air, on the dock in front of Arthur's boat.

Arthur glanced up and over his shoulder. Rex stood on the roof, hands in the air, Ferro's hired help pressing a gun in his back.

Rex raised his hand in front of his chest and quickly pointed toward the Intracoastal, then held up five fingers, made a fist, and held up three.

Backup was eight minutes out.

All Arthur had to do was remain cool for the longest eight minutes of his life.

The goon pushed Arthur toward the dock.

"So, what's the plan?" Arthur asked.

"You're going to die, that's the plan," the goon said.

"How?"

"Shut the fuck up before I hit you again."

"Don't you think it's only fair—"

Smack!

Arthur's head jerked to the side when the goon's fist landed on his cheek.

"Motherfucker."

"Keep talking, asshole, and I'll keep using you as a punching bag."

Well, that took up maybe forty-five seconds.

The sound of Rex dragging his feet echoed behind Arthur. He wanted to turn around and tell Rex to pick his fucking feet up. It drove Arthur nuts when Rex was too lazy to walk like a normal person.

The dragging got louder.

"Jesus, Rex. Walk much?"

"I'll walk however I like, especially when you might get me killed, jackass."

"You're not dead, yet," Arthur said as his feet

hit the dock, eyeing his other buddies as their captors loaded them onto his boat.

Down to five minutes.

Arthur cleared his mind. He hated not knowing other people's plans, and right now, all he knew was that Maren's life was in someone else's hands.

He stopped in front of his boat slip and blinked, letting the reality of the situation sink in.

He smiled.

Kent, Duncan, Buddy, and the two men he thought had been Ferro's goons had turned out to be Hawke and Garth, who all held assault rifles.

The goon holding Arthur's biceps held his weapon up.

"I'd put that down if I were you," Kent said, pointing his gun to Rex's yacht. "We've got this place surrounded."

"Now help our buddies onto the boat and hand over your weapons," Buddy said.

Arthur didn't wait for any help. "Get this shit off me." He jumped onto the bow, holding his hands out. Duncan quickly cut through the tie, handing him a weapon.

"Hold that for one second." He grabbed the goon that had hit him. "Payback is a bitch." He clenched his right hand into a tight fist and jabbed the asshole in the nose.

Rex caught the goon before he fell backward into the water.

"And you." Arthur pointed at Rex. "You said eight minutes out."

Rex shrugged. "I didn't know they were here already."

"We got a problem," Kent said, pointing toward the office. "They know we're here."

Arthur stepped onto the dock and sucked in a deep breath.

Ferro hid behind Maren and her mother as they made their way toward Gretchen's sport SUV. Ferro held a gun to Maren's temple.

"Does anyone have a clean shot?" Arthur yelled.

"We're firefighters, not snipers," Rex said, his weapon raised. Of all of them, Rex was probably the best shot. "Not going to happen, but I can blow out the tire—"

Bang!

"Fuck me." Rex groaned, dropping to his knees, clutching his thigh. "Arthur, you're gonna pay for this."

"I didn't shoot you." Arthur took off running,

weaving between the boats as Ferro took a couple of potshots.

A few shots rang out from behind him as one of his buddies blew out two tires. The sound of boots hitting wood echoed. His heart thumped against his chest in a painful beat. The only man not accounted for was Jefferson, a thought that disturbed him as he ran out onto the open pavement, waiting for Jefferson to appear from the main building, gun at the ready.

Arthur clutched his weapon with one hand, digging into his pockets for his keys. They couldn't have gotten too far ahead, but if they made it to the first intersection, he'd have to guess their direction.

He'd barely shut the truck door when he rammed the gear shift into drive and punched the gas, fishtailing. Off in the distance, he heard sirens.

Taking the turn onto the main road, he saw Gretchen's car make the left turn at the first light. He slammed the gas pedal, banging his fist on the center of the wheel as he passed two cars. Red lights flashed a few miles down the road.

He took the corner, the wheels on the right side of his pickup lifting slightly off the ground. No sooner did he straighten out, gaining control of the vehicle, than he saw the sport SUV spinning out of control.

Crash!

It slammed into a tree, sending it into the air before flipping it upside down.

Arthur's heart dropped to his gut as he raced toward the car. A spark sizzled and crackled as flames erupted. He snagged his fire extinguisher and doused what he could. Kneeling beside the car, careful not to get glass stuck in his knees, he peered inside.

"Arthur," Gretchen moaned, her body hanging from the front seat, her seat belt holding her in place.

"I need to get you out of here." Arthur saw Ferro crawling from the driver's side. Nothing he could about him right now.

Tires screeched behind him as a police car pulled to the side of the road. He glanced over his shoulder to see Rusty leap from the vehicle.

"Get Ferro." Arthur turned his attention to the back seat. His chest tightened, squeezing out all the air in his lungs. Maren lay on the roof of the car, her body twisted, and blood tinged her clothes.

"Help Maren."

"I will, but let's get you out of here first. Do you hurt anywhere?"

She shook her head, her hands fisting his shirt. "My daughter."

"Ferro is secure," Rusty said, taking the fire extinguisher. "Ambulance is ten minutes out. Fire engine six."

He had no idea the extent of Maren's injuries, but it didn't look good. He blinked, forcing himself to focus on getting them out.

"Hold on to my shoulders, okay?" He reached around Gretchen's body, grabbing hold of the seat belt.

Flames continued to flicker, and the smell of gas once again filled his nostrils.

"Tuck your head into my shoulder. I'm going to release this on the count of three and you'll fall, but I'm going to catch you. One, two, three." He tugged at the metal clasp. Her body plunged into his arms as she gripped his shoulders.

Black smoke filled the sky as he ran toward his truck, setting her gently in the passenger seat.

"Oh my God," Gretchen whispered.

"Stay right here, don't move."

Arthur's pulse soared out of control. He

climbed into the back seat, feeling Maren's body for any broken bones.

She moaned, rolling her head.

"Maren, sweetheart, can you hear me?" he asked. Nothing appeared to be broken, but again, there was no way of knowing what kind of damage had been done internally.

He pressed his fingers against her wrist. Her pulse was slow and weak.

"Maren, honey. Wake up." He reached down, lifting her eyelid. He swallowed. Hard.

"Arthur, you've got to get her out of there now. This tank is about empty, and the fire is kicking up."

He slid his arms under her body, ignoring the searing pain of glass ripping through his skin. He coughed as the black, oily smoke filled his lungs. Careful not to jostle her too much, he inched his way out of the vehicle just as the fire engine rolled down the street.

"Maren!" her mother called as she hopped out of the truck. "Is she okay?"

Arthur turned his body, protecting Maren's. "I need to keep her as still as possible." Tears stung the corners of his eyes. With each rise of her chest, a faint gurgling sound filtered from her lips.

"Why? What's wrong with my little one?"

He held Maren in his arms, his lips pressed against her forehead. Her skin was cold and clammy to the touch.

Firemen shouted in the background. The spray from the hoses floated down on him like the mist from a car wash. The paramedics rolled out the gurney.

"I think she has a punctured lung," he said as he stretched her out on the backboard. "I hear gurgling. Her pulse is weak. She's cold, clammy, and unresponsive."

"What?" Gretchen cried out, reaching for her daughter.

"Step back, ma'am," the paramedic said, pushing the gurney toward the ambulance.

"That's my daughter," Gretchen said.

"Let them do their jobs," Arthur said, raising his arm to wrap it around Gretchen, but he thought better of it when he saw all the blood.

Another paramedic approached them. "I think we need to take a look at both of you."

"Start with her." Arthur sighed.

"I want to be with my daughter," Gretchen protested.

The paramedic pointed toward the first ambulance. "They are transporting her to the hospital now. Let us check you over, assess any injuries, and we'll make sure we keep you updated on your daughter's condition."

"Arthur?"

He squeezed her shoulder. "Let them take you to the hospital. I'll be along shortly."

Arthur wiped his eyes as he marched across the road where paramedics were attending to Ferro.

Arthur bent over Ferro and grabbed him by the shirt. "You're a fucking piece of shit."

"Let go of me," Ferro said.

Arthur released one hand and fisted the other one.

Crack!

The first swing hit Ferro on the cheekbone.

Smash!

The second landed square on Ferro's nose.

"Might want to have that nose checked out. Looks broken."

"That was uncalled for," Rusty said.

"Yeah, but it felt really fucking fantastic."

11

Arthur held Maren's hand as he rested his forehead on the hospital bed. Medical equipment beeped in the background. IV bags hung from a metal post, pumping fluids and medicine into her veins. An oxygen tube was in her nose.

The broken ribs would heal.

The punctured lung would mend.

But it had been three days since the accident, and Maren had yet to wake up.

"Arthur," Gretchen's voice rang out soft and sweet. "You didn't sleep here again, did you?" Her warm hands came down on his shoulders. "You really should go home for a few hours."

"I'll go home when she wakes up."

"I know you care very much for my daughter, but really, you're not going to do her any good if you end up getting sick because you're so run-down from not taking care of yourself."

He reached up, patting her strong hand. "I'd be in worse shape if I left."

"You're a good man."

He hoped... prayed he'd get the chance to prove he was good enough to have Maren on his arm.

"Anything happen overnight?" Gretchen asked.

"Not really. They said the swelling in her brain is down," he said, lifting his head, watching Gretchen tug and pull at the sheets.

"That's a good sign." Gretchen moved to the other side of the bed, stroking Maren's hair.

The cuts and bruises had started to heal, and she looked peaceful.

"Have you had anything to eat since last night?" Gretchen asked.

"I'm not that hungry."

She shook her head. "I'll go get you something."

"You don't have to do that. Really. I'll get something later."

Maren's hand twitched in his.

He stood up. "Maren?" he whispered.

Her eyelids fluttered.

"Maren, sweetheart," he said a little louder.

Her head rolled to the side.

"I'll go get the doctor." Gretchen shuffled out of the room.

Arthur's pulse raced. His hand trembled as he reached out and cupped her cheek. "That's it, honey, open those beautiful eyes."

"Arthur?" she asked with a raspy voice. "Where am I?"

"In the hospital."

She tried to lift up her head and groaned. "My head feels like a bomb exploded."

"Shhhhh." He kissed her forehead. "You've been asleep for a few days with a concussion."

"A few days?"

Before he could explain what happened, the doctor and a nurse came in.

Arthur stepped back, leaning against the windowsill, tears threatening to break free, while the doctor examined Maren.

The doctor asked a series of questions, and Maren answered them all. Other than her physical injuries and a whopper of a headache, she seemed to be just fine.

A tear rolled down his cheek. He turned toward the window and quickly wiped it away. He wasn't going to break down in front of them. They needed his strength.

"You're looking good," the doctor said. "I'm going to keep you here another day or two, just to make sure."

From the moment Arthur had looked at her in the bait and tackle store, she'd been under his skin, worming her way into his psyche. The first time he'd pulled her from a wreck had been intense as a life was at stake.

But the second time, his heart was on the line and now he had to find a way to show her how much he cared and wanted her in his life.

"If you feel nauseous or disoriented at all, please hit the nurse call button, okay?" the doctor said.

"I will," Maren said as her mother helped her to a sitting position. "Can I eat something?"

The doctor laughed. "Being hungry is an excellent sign. Until dinner, all we have here is Jell-O and pudding."

Maren scrunched her nose.

"I can get you something from the cafeteria," her mother said.

"Peanut butter toast would be great."

"You always loved that when you were sick as a little girl." Her mother patted Maren's leg. "I'll go see what I can find."

"I'll go to the cafeteria," Arthur said. "Would you like anything, Gretchen?"

"Coffee would be great." Gretchen squeezed his biceps. "You're a good man, Arthur. I don't know what we would have done without you."

He leaned in and kissed her cheek, his heart thick with emotion. "I'll be back in a jiffy." He stepped into the hallway, pausing once out of the wing. He leaned against the wall by the elevators and took a long breath.

His eyes burned and he couldn't stop the tears that poured. He snagged his cell from his back pocket and found Darius' contact information.

It rang once.

"Hey, man, how are you holding up? How's Maren?" Darius asked.

"She's awake," Arthur said. "The doctor says she's no worse for the wear."

"That's excellent news. I'm sure her mother is as relieved as you sound. Only, I can tell there's something in your voice that's got you all twisted up. What's wrong?"

"I should be jumping up and down for joy. Ferro's behind bars and he's not getting out. Justice for Sarah and her family is finally being served. Gretchen doesn't have to worry and she and the marina will be fine."

"Ah. I get it now. You don't know where you fit in Maren's world. If she's coming or going."

"Something like that," Arthur said. "I didn't want to feel like this again. I've successfully avoided it for years. But her life is in New York."

"Jesus, man. Aren't you the one who told me she quit her job and dumped her loser boyfriend."

Arthur chuckled. "Both true. But that doesn't mean she's coming back here and it's not like I can ask her to stay right after—"

"Of course you can," Darius said. "Don't be an asshole. Give her a day or two to catch her breath and tell her how you feel. Otherwise, you're going to let the best thing that ever happened to you walk right out of your life because you've got shit for balls when it comes to your emotions."

"I don't want to come on too strong. She's already called me out on being a controlling prick."

"You're such a dumbass sometimes," Darius said. "There's a difference between barking orders at someone and being honest. One of these days you'll figure it out. Hopefully, before she gives up on you."

"I wouldn't want that to happen." He pushed from the wall and hit the elevator button. "I gotta go get her some toast and her mom some coffee. I'll talk with you later."

"Don't fuck this up, or I'll have to fly out there and beat the crap out of you."

"Like that's possible."

"Catch you later."

Arthur stepped into the elevator. His old friend was right. He needed to give Maren a few days. She'd been through a lot physically and emotionally. Once she was back at home, he'd tell her what he was feeling and what he wanted.

Maybe she wanted the same thing.

"Can I have some water, Mom?" Maren shifted in the hospital bed. Every inch of her body ached. Her head felt as if something exploded.

"Of course, little one." Her mom handed her a Styrofoam cup with a straw. She took a napkin and blotted her cheeks. "It's been a long few days."

"I'm sorry."

"You're awake now and that bastard and all his buddies are going to jail, thanks to Arthur and his friends." Her mother patted her leg. "You should know that this is the first time Arthur has left your side since we brought you to the hospital. He's been such a mess. I've never seen him so worried."

Maren blew out a puff of air. Her heart swelled. "I'm sure he went home at some point."

Her mother shook her head. "No, little one. I would leave in the evening, and when I came back in the morning, he would still be right in that chair, holding your hand. I've tried to get him to go home, but he wouldn't. I've tried to get him to eat, but he hasn't touched a thing. About the only thing I could get him to do was change his clothes."

So many things raced through her mind. Arthur had a heart of gold. Even his controlling ways had grown on her, but only because she knew that when he cared, he cared with every fiber of his being. She'd only known him for a short time. However, it felt like a lifetime.

She had no idea if that was good or bad.

But what she did know was she wanted more time with Arthur.

"He insisted I get my rest," her mother said. "He told me that if there was a change, he'd call me. While I do believe he wanted me to take care of myself, I also think he couldn't bring himself to leave the hospital until he knew you were okay."

"That's a lot to take in," Maren whispered.

"He cares about you." Her mother sat on the edge of the bed and took her hand. "I know I pushed Arthur on you. But all I wanted was for the two of you to meet. I can't force people to like each other." She lowered her chin. "I can see it in his eyes how he feels about you. But right now, all I see in yours in confusion."

"Oh, Mom. I'm not confused about how I feel. I obviously like Arthur a lot. I don't know what to make of it all. Or my life. I came home to help you figure out the next steps with the marina. We're still in that boat."

"You know what I really want, little one. I wish you did too."

Maren smiled. "There's only one thing that I know for sure and that's that I have no desire to go back to New York."

"You mean that?" Her mother blinked.

"Yeah, Mom. I mean it. My lease for my apartment is up in a month and I'm not going to renew it." Maren held up her hand. "I'd like to move back into the family home. As far as the marina's concerned, let's see how things go for the next few months. Okay?"

"That's a deal I can live with."

"Just promise me you won't say anything to Arthur. That's my job."

"My lips are sealed," her mother said.

Now all she had to get was get up the nerve to take the next step and lay her heart on the line.

12

Arthur finished the last of the dishes, grateful that Maren and her mom let him cook them dinner on Maren's first night home.

"Hey, Arthur," Gretchen called as she peeked her head inside from the porch.

"What's up?"

"I'm going to go see my friend down the street. Maren would like a glass of wine. Do you mind bringing her one?"

"Not at all," he said.

"Jackie and I have lots to gossip about." She waggled her finger. "So, I expect you to have some vino with my little one and enjoy the night."

He laughed. "Yes, ma'am." He snagged two

glasses and a bottle before heading outside. "Hey, you."

"Hey, yourself." Maren leaned against the railing. "It's a beautiful evening. Look at all the stars."

"When I was a little boy, my dad used to take me out on the boat at night and we'd drop over a few lines. Then we'd lie back and count the stars in the sky. Sometimes we'd get so distracted by it that'd we'd lose a good fish." He poured the wine, handing her a glass.

"Your dad sounds like quite the guy. I hope I get to meet him sometime."

"He and my sister are coming next month for a week." He took a long slow sip before setting his glass on the railing. "You gave me quite the scare."

She set aside her glass and took his hand. "I guess I owe you once again for saving my life."

"I might let you take me out to dinner this time."

"Oh, really?"

He nodded. "Not sure I'll let you pay, but you can pick the restaurant." He lowered his gaze, taking in a long breath. "And I don't want one dinner. Or even two. I want to toss in a few breakfasts and a romantic stroll on the beach."

"Romantic?" she questioned. "Do you know what that word means?"

He chuckled. "I might have a basic understanding of the concept."

"This I'd like to see."

He swallowed. Time for all or nothing. "I don't want you to go back to New York. I've gotten used to having you around."

"Oh." She smiled. "As in you want me to be a permanent fixture in your life?"

He traced her lower lip with his index finger. "I want to explore the possibility."

"Wow," she whispered. "Those are some big words for a man like you."

"Too much, too quick?"

"No," she said. "Crazy, but I want that too. However, let's start with a couple of nice dinners."

"Name the time and place."

Her smile brightened the night sky and made his heart flutter with anticipation. "You'll have to drive because all our family cars are toast and even though I've talked to my mom about what she wants, she's a pain in the ass when it comes to buying one."

He shook his head. "What is it with you and burning cars?"

The corners of her mouth tipped upward. "I just wanted to see a sexy firefighter in action."

"You were unconscious."

"But you did pull me from the wreckage."

He nodded. "Though I would appreciate it if you never make me do that again." He tapped his chest. "I don't think my heart could take it."

"I'll try not to, but only on one condition."

"Yeah, what's that?"

"You kiss me right now, because I've had a burning desire to feel your lips on mine since the second my mom left."

EPILOGUE

SIX MONTHS LATER...

Arthur raised the longneck to his lips, sipping the bitter brew as he stared at Maren sitting in the bow of his boat, reading a book while Shasta slowly thumped her tail. The sun beat down on the calm ocean, his vessel rocking gently with the rolling waves. The last six months had been the best of his life. His career was perfect.

And he was lucky enough to have the love of the perfect woman.

"I can feel you staring at me," Maren said. The sweet timbre of her voice floated across the air, blanketing his skin like the stars did the sky.

He chuckled. "That's because you're the prettiest thing out here."

"Flattery will get you whatever you want."

"Whatever I want?" He cocked his head.

She peered over her book. "Why do I feel like I'm being baited?"

"You said anything." He tipped his beer.

"What's on your mind?"

He waggled his finger at her. "Come here and I'll show you what's on my mind." He patted his lap.

"We are not having sex on this boat in broad daylight. Besides, it would traumatize the dog." She pushed herself to a standing position, and holding on to the side of the boat, she slinked her way to the center console, then straddled his lap. "Don't get any ideas. I'm just here for the beer." She took the bottle from his hand, her lips covering the glass opening, and chugged half of it. "Mmmm, that hit the spot."

"You're such a tease." He curled his hands over her hips.

She smiled.

"I love you," he whispered. He'd felt those words for longer than he'd been saying them, but it still humbled him every time he spoke them.

"I love you too, but now I really know you're up

to something." She glanced around. "Usually means a prank or some weird, wicked joke."

"You'll never learn to be quiet, will you." He swallowed the lump in his throat. "I was thinking."

"About?"

"Us."

She tilted her head. "What about us?"

"I think we should get a dog." Not how he planned on starting this conversation, but it would work.

He hoped.

"We have a dog."

He laughed. "I mean a dog that lives with us full-time."

"We don't live together, and Shasta does live with me full-time."

Shasta's head popped up as she yelped.

He arched his brow.

"You're serious?"

"I hate sneaking out of your mother's house and getting caught nine times out of ten, and I hate it when you leave my apartment. I just think it would better all around if you moved in with me."

"I'll move in with you."

He coughed. "Really?"

"On one condition."

"I bet I can guess what that is." Though he had no idea, but if he didn't do this now, he might lose his nerve.

"I doubt that," she said.

He patted her ass. "Get up."

"You're being bossy and you know how I feel about that."

He flipped open the compartment on the console and pulled out a small pouch. "I bet your condition on shacking up is that we get married."

"That's not what I was going to say."

He dumped the engagement ring into his hand and got down on one knee. Might as well do this right. "Marry me."

"Is that a demand? Because you know I can't stand it when you get all controlling and shit on me."

He growled. "As your future husband, I will just warn you that I will be demanding on a regular basis."

She took the ring in her hand. "What caramel candy popcorn box did you get this from? Is Rex out there taking a video somewhere? The things you think are funny are really just weird. I mean, come on, if this is one of your silly jokes and—"

"You really need to learn to stop jumping to

conclusions and just listen to me." He snagged the ring as he stood up and wiggled it on her finger. "Real ring. Real proposal. So, what's it going to be? Marriage and a dog? Or shall I just jump in the water and put myself out of my misery?"

She glanced between the ring and him with wide eyes. "Really, real? As in a real diamond ring?"

He let out an exasperated sigh and nodded.

A slow smile drew across her face. "What I was going to say was that if you want me to move in, we've got to get a bigger place than your apartment."

"That's a no-brainer. They don't allow large dogs."

"Well, future husband, looks like you're going to get your wish."

He kissed her hand. "Good. Now let me get back to fishing."

"That's not the wish I was talking about. I mean, yeah, I'll marry you, but I was agreeing to have sex with you right here, right now."

Thank you for reading *Arthur's Honor.* Next up is *Rex's Honor.* If you'd like to know more about Darius Ford, please check out: ***Darius' Promise***

. . .

Grab a glass of vino, kick back, relax, and let the romance roll in…

Sign up for my Newsletter (https://dl.bookfunnel.com/82gm8b9k4y) where I often give away free books before publication.

Join my private Facebook group (https://www.facebook.com/groups/191706547909047/) where I post exclusive excerpts and discuss all things murder and love!

Never miss a new release. Follow me on Amazon:amazon.com/author/jentalty

And on Bookbub: bookbub.com/authors/jentalty

ABOUT THE AUTHOR

Jen Talty is the *USA Today* Bestselling Author of Contemporary Romance, Romantic Suspense, and Paranormal Romance. In the fall of 2020, her short story was selected and featured in a 1001 Dark Nights Anthology.

Regardless of the genre, her goal is to take you on a ride that will leave you floating under the sun with warmth in your heart. She writes stories about broken heroes and heroines who aren't necessarily looking for romance, but in the end, they find the kind of love books are written about :).

She first started writing while carting her kids to one hockey rink after the other, averaging 170 games per year between 3 kids in 2 countries and 5 states. Her first book, IN TWO WEEKS was originally published in 2007. In 2010 she helped form a publishing company (Cool Gus Publishing) with *NY*

Times Bestselling Author Bob Mayer where she ran the technical side of the business through 2016.

Jen is currently enjoying the next phase of her life…the empty nester! She and her husband reside in Jupiter, Florida.

Grab a glass of vino, kick back, relax, and let the romance roll in…

    Sign up for my Newsletter (https://dl.bookfunnel.com/82gm8b9k4y). where I often give away free books before publication.

Join my private Facebook group (https://www.facebook.com/groups/191706547909047/) where I post exclusive excerpts and discuss all things murder and love!

Never miss a new release. Follow me on Amazon:amazon.com/author/jentalty

    And on Bookbub: bookbub.com/authors/jen-talty

ALSO BY JEN TALTY

Brand new series: SAFE HARBOR!

Mine To Keep

Mine To Save

Mine To Protect

Mine to Hold

Mine to Love

Check out LOVE IN THE ADIRONDACKS!

Shattered Dreams

An Inconvenient Flame

The Wedding Driver

Clear Blue Sky

Blue Moon

Before the Storm

NY STATE TROOPER SERIES (also set in the Adirondacks!)

In Two Weeks

Dark Water

Burning Bed

Remember Me Always

The Brotherhood Protectors

Out of the Wild

Rough Justice

Rough Around The Edges

Rough Ride

Rough Edge

Rough Beauty

The Brotherhood Protectors

The Saving Series

Saving Love

Saving Magnolia

Saving Leather

Hot Hunks

Cove's Blind Date Blows Up

My Everyday Hero – Ledger

Tempting Tavor

Malachi's Mystic Assignment

Needing Neor